A Walk in the Abyss

by

Paul Genesse

Shane Moore

Patrick M. Tracy

Patrick S. Tomlinson

This is a work of fiction. All of the characters, organizations, and events portrayed in this book are either products of the authors' imaginations or are used fictitiously.

A WALK IN THE ABYSS

© Shane Moore

A New Babel Books Release

www.newbabelbooks.com

ISBN: 978-1-63196-031-4

Printed in the United States of America.

No-Tusks written by and © 2013 Paul Genesse

A Kudekah to Remember written by and © 2013 Shane Moore and Paul Genesse

Mungo the Undying by written by and © 2013 Patrick M. Tracy

Unerring written by and © 2013 Patrick S. Tomlinson

The Wererat's Tale III: A Collar and Perdition written by and © 2013 Patrick S. Tomlinson

The Abyss Walker World © Shane Moore

Cover art by and © 2013 Dan Harding

Interior art by and © 2013 Zachary Hill

Graphic Design and Interior art by and © 2013 Kendall R. Hart

TABLE OF CONTENTS

INTRODUCTION

Orcs! Greyshalks! And Giants! Oh my!

Prepare yourselves, intrepid reader, for three complete novelettes set in the Abyss Walker world of author Shane Moore. In this anthology you shall read "No Tusks" by Paul Genesse, the disgustingly graphic orc story—not for children—(You have been warned!); then a tale about a young Sasquatch, or more accurately, a greyshalk trying to find his place in the world in: "A Kudekah to Remember" by Paul Genesse and Shane Moore; and finally, a truly hilarious story about a bumbling giant in: "Mungo the Undying" by Patrick M. Tracy. You'll also be treated to a short story from a very unique point of view—an arrow in flight: "Unerring" by Patrick S. Tomlinson; and as a bonus, an excerpt from the novella, "The Wererat's Tale III: The Collar of Perdition" by Patrick S. Tomlinson, which was written from an outline penned by the creator of the Abyss Walker World, Shane Moore himself. Orcs, greyshalks, and giants (and wererats) will never be the same!

No-Tusks
by Paul Genesse

The smell of roasted dog made Tezok's mouth water. The taste of meat had been denied the young orc for many days as he survived on bird eggs and a handful of mushrooms he'd scavenged in the freezing forest. His yellow eyes peered beyond the leaning trunks of dead oak trees to the source of the enticing smell, now tainted with the old sour blood scent of his own kind.

Fear of being alone in the forest—and a desperate hunger—drove him to creep toward the red-orange firelight and spy on the small war party of orcs. They were the first that he had seen since fleeing his own tribe. He knew that no matter how clever he might be, one small orc in the elf-infested forest near the Minok Vale during Winter would not see the Spring.

His mind made up, Tezok prayed silently to the Angry God Drunda, promising to make many blood offerings if these orcs would take him into their tribe. After urinating on himself to show a proper amount of fear, he crawled on all fours and whimpered as he entered the campsite. The lone guard grabbed him by his knotted mass of greasy black hair, dragged him into the center of their circle, and threw him down hard on the ground.

"Why is runt skulking into Kar-Pok's camp?" The largest orc, the Kar of the war party displayed his long yellow tusks as he sniffed the air. "Runt not much bigger than a whelp."

"Runt is food for march," the guard said, causing grins, which looked like an exaggeration of the orcs' already-large underbites.

"Not food. I slave. Let slave serve great Iron Spear tribe."

The Kar clicked his tusks against his sharp upper teeth, his surprise only half-hidden. "You know of Iron Spear tribe?"

"All of Drunda's spawn know Iron Spear tribe and ferocious leader, Kar-Pok, who is Elf-Killer and Cattle-Stealer."

The orcs laughed and Kar-Pok swelled up his chest, failing to realize that the young orc might have heard the war leader mention his tribe's name as he boasted of his prowess moments before.

"Kar-Pok!" The large orc slammed a fist against his muscled chest covered. Then his green-skinned hand — coated with dog's blood — wrapped around the young orc's throat. Kar-Pok pushed his small captive against a flat stone beside the fire where they'd butchered the dog.

"No. Not food." The whimpering orc's left tusk grated against the rock as Kar-Pok opened his free hand, motioning for a weapon. One of the warriors slapped the handle of a rusty hatchet into it.

"Not food. Good slave. I serve Kar-Pok." Overwhelming terror made Tezok squirm and fight. He cursed himself for entering the camp. It would have been better to die alone than end up as meat.

Kar-Pok raised the hatchet despite the whimpering and the sincere stream of urine that began to muddy the ground.

"We see if you good slave." Kar-Pok chopped downward, shattering Tezok's left tusk. After two more whacks he turned him over, pressing the squealing orc's square jaw against the rock. Kar-Pok held him still as he broke the other tusk with repeated blows, first with the sharp edge, then with the flat side of the hatchet head, each blow more excruciating than the last.

"*Ukluk! Ukluk!*" The orcs shouted as they howled into the night. "*Ukluk kech garga!*"

The blinding, throbbing pain from losing his tusks made Tezok's new name even worse. *Ukluk,* the humiliated and emasculated young orc thought bitterly as he swallowed the blood filling in his mouth. No female would ever mate with him if he didn't have tusks. It would have been better if he had been killed by the elves.

He curled into a ball as the warriors kicked him and prodded him with burning logs from the fire. As he endured the attacks, the pain and fear became a red-hot desire for vengeance. Let them call him whatever they wanted. He would bide his time, and use the witch Valga's secret knowledge to get back at them. When the moment came, he would show them who he really was and have his revenge on Kar-Pok and entire Iron Spear tribe. Until then, he would be the lowliest wretch, and they would call him No-Tusks the Slave.

Ukluk sucked the worm from Kar-Pok's muddy foot, ignoring the stagnant swamp water latrine taste. With good pressure he could get the head of the worm to poke out of the surface, then he could nip it carefully with his lips and pull out its entire body. The war leader and now the chief of the Iron Spear tribe's feet did not taste as bad as some of the others, and Ukluk went about his duty with dogged determination. His strong effort quickly yielded a prize as a gelatinous, but gritty white worm came out with a pop. Ukluk chewed up the bitter morsel and swallowed, then found the entry point where another had burrowed into Kar-Pok's fungus-covered foot.

The raiding party of twelve orcs would soon depart, long before midnight if the war ceremony went well. They had a tough march ahead of them if they would find the herd of cattle Ukluk told Kar-Pok he had discovered a few days before when he scouted the plains of Beykla. The report of such a large herd thankfully distracted Kar-Pok enough that he did not ask what had kept Ukluk away for so long. The chief had no clue that three years of scheming and planning by his lowly slave were about to change the Iron Spear tribe forever. The pleasant thought made Ukluk stop sucking out a worm from the chief's heel, allowing the bloodsucking creature to slip back inside.

Kar-Pok had not been paying attention, but when the slave paused, the chief noticed the bee sting bulging like a red berry on the tip of Ukluk's pointed ear. The chief grabbed Ukluk's injured ear and painfully lifted him up, pinching the bee sting hard. "Slave cross swamp and find honey?"

"No," Ukluk lied. If they found out where he had been his plan could be ruined. All the bee hives in their territory had been raided and no orc in the tribe dared go to the forest on the other side of the swamp where Mungo, the red haired man-giant, lived. If they knew Ukluk had been going onto the giant's land and pretending to be a messenger from Kar-Pok, the chief would kill Ukluk for certain.

"No-Tusks lies," Kar-Pok said, pinching the sting harder. "Where No-Tusks find hive?"

"On plains," Ukluk said, "near cattle herd, but humans take hive honey before No-Tusks find it. No-Tusks sorry he fail to gather honey for Kar-Pok."

The chief smashed Ukluk in the face with a knee, then stomped on the little orc's hands while he lay stunned on the ground. "Next time No-Tusks scout, he finds hive before humans and comes back sooner."

Ukluk nodded as he whimpered and licked the chief's feet, hoping Kar-Pok would not beat him too severely. Instead of hitting him, the chief lanced the bee sting on Ukluk's ear with the tip of a dagger, causing hoots of laughter from the warriors. It was a small injury, and nothing compared to the suffering he'd endured before. After each scouting trip the chief would beat Ukluk for being gone, though it was the

Kar-Pok who had sent him away to search for food or plunder.

Despite the certain pain he would suffer when he returned, Ukluk found that scouting was his favorite task. Not only was he able to get away from the constant torment inflicted upon him by every orc in the tribe, Ukluk could gather the healing plants and poisonous mushrooms that the orc witch, Valga, had told him about. His time studying with her seemed like a lifetime ago. If only she had not angered the chief of their tribe, forcing her to flee for her life with her dumb and ugly blue-eyed whelp, Vlarcar. Ukluk would have stayed, and maybe someday he could have become the mouthpiece of the tribe, even if he was of the *garga* caste. Valga would have taught him the dark magic and tattooed his hide with the protections she had placed upon her son. It wasn't a likely outcome, he had to admit, but if he was the only one who knew the secret knowledge of the Angry God and was skilled in the ways of making Drunda's poisons, there might have been a chance.

In the Iron Spear tribe, he had no hope of being accepted as the equal of a warrior. Even if he revealed that he possessed Drunda's secret poison knowledge, Ukluk was the smallest and weakest male orc by far, only four and half feet tall. He could never be more than a slave. The males were huge, the females were all bigger and tougher than him, and even a few of the older whelps could look him evenly in his bloodshot eyes.

Ukluk finished with the chief's feet and rubbed

lye all over them to kill the fungus and whatever else was growing. He immediately started on the second in command. Torgash's feet stunk like he had soaked them in a bog filled with dead skunks for an entire summer. Three of Torgash's toes were greenish black and the gangrenous stench made Ukluk wrinkle his snout. He took a moment to wipe some of the fresh cow dung he'd gathered from the herd into his nostrils, then began his task. At least the manure had a pleasant odor. Kar-Pok had thought so as well. The chief had demanded to taste and smell it when Ukluk had returned with a handful.

"This cow is well fed," Kar-Pok said as he sucked on the moist dung that he kept tucked inside his cheek. "Humans have fed them oats."

"How many cattle?" Torgash asked.

Ukluk thought for a long moment. He did not want to confuse, and thereby anger Torgash, who would not understand the man words, *one hundred*, which some orc tribes had come to use as their language lacked terms or gestures for such large numbers. "If every orc in Iron Spear tribe had three cows, that is how big herd is."

Torgash's mouth hung open, his rotten teeth and black tongue on display as he salivated.

"How many humans watch cattle?" Kar-Pok asked.

Ukluk held up three fingers on each hand. "Some whelps, others had too many winters. Few blooded warriors."

"What weapons they hold?" Kar-Pok asked.

"Bows, axes, knives. No swords. No armor,"

Ukluk said.

"We'll kill them all," Torgash said, his tusks jutting forward as he raised his large battle-axe.

The war party joked and boasted about how they would slaughter the humans as Ukluk worked to complete his task. Once he was done with the war party's feet, he followed the chief's instructions and gave each of the warriors a single fire mushroom to use in the upcoming battle. The red mushrooms would make them even stronger and more resistant to pain. He also gave them a cup of bog wine to drink before they left, and an empty pouch to carry back battle trophies or loot.

All of the adult male orcs and some of the older whelps began to gather around the chief as the final preparations were made. They formed a circle and knelt down, the strongest closer to Kar-Pok in the center, while the whelps sat furthest away, and Ukluk even further—as befit his caste.

"While warriors go kill humans and steal cattle," Kar-Pok said, "Vrishnek is Kar."

"Kar-Vrishnek!" Vrishnek raised his one good arm. The other was still weak from the wound he'd suffered from a human farmer with an axe. The man had died defending his small tribe of whelps and women. It was Vrishnek who had killed the axe man and gained the right to be the first to taste his blood.

Two other wounded orcs, who had been hurt on a different raid, were in much worse shape. Meglarg had lost an eye and could barely walk as he was recovering from a wound to his thigh. Feglak had been pierced through the forehead by crossbow bolt and was half the warrior he had been before the injury. The large and ferocious orc had lost the ability to lift his war hammer over his head, or hold down even the smallest of the females.

As the tribe's only trained healer, Ukluk had deemed it best to saw off the protruding shaft and leave the rest of the bolt and the tip inside Feglak's brain. To protect him from further injury, Ukluk had screwed a small circular plate of iron into Feglak's skull. Only the Angry God knew if Feglak would recover his prowess, and since Feglak was the tribe's best gate-smasher, Kar-Pok had allowed him to live—for now.

Five whelps came bounding out of the cave. They had smeared their naked bodies with ash, ochre mud, and fresh blood. All of them were armed with clubs and a few had elf- or dwarf-skin drums. The slower whelps in the back beat the smaller ones in the front with their drum-clubs and howled curses. They stopped their shouting when Kar-Pok's angry yellow eyes fell upon them.

"Iron Spear tribe stays near cave while warriors raiding," Kar-Pok's words fell like boulders. "Stay quiet while we are gone." He glared at the whelps. "Hide in cave. Kill any who enter cave with log trap, then barricade tribe inside. If Iron Spear have to flee, crawl out escape-holes. Take clan totem, females, and oldest whelps. Leave the squealing milk-suckers and Feglak behind as a distraction."

Feglak heard his name and turned around, trying to figure out who said it.

"Carry as much meat as tribe can if all must flee lair," the chief said. "Iron Spear tribe will gather on Leech Island in swamp. Meet there."

"Tribe won't hide or flee." Vrishnek wrinkled his snout and bit an oak branch in half, causing many of the orcs to laugh.

Kar-Pok punched him in the jaw, staggering the wounded orc. Vrishnek stood with a grin and punched Kar-Pok, not quite as hard, right in his stubby snout, which leaked a few drops of blood. The two orcs grinned, their tusks turned up at the moon as they shouted at each other, *"Brohe-tah!"*

The war party howled. They joined the whelps and began pounding the drums, or banging their weapons against their piecemeal armor or shields. After several moments of furious drumming, Kar-Pok spotted Ukluk, who had been hiding behind a rock hoping not to draw the attention of the tribe, which was becoming more and more enraged by the moment. "Slave! Bring totem Iron Spear."

Ukluk scurried toward the entrance to the caverns. He caught the faint scent of the females, who almost always hid themselves when the warrior males were around. He did not have to duck his head like all of the other full-grown orcs as he entered. Still he paused, allowing his pupils to dilate to the size of iron pennies, which allowed him to see every detail in the darkness. The deadly log trap guarded the passage, and Ukluk made certain it was not sagging downward, appearing as if it would fall on him. The trap looked secure, unmolested by the whelps, though he would check the ropes later that night when there were no prying eyes.

Over forty heavy logs had been lashed together and lined up, twenty on either side of the cave, disguised to look like they were propping up the ceiling by forming a sharp-peaked roof. Hundreds of metal and wooden spikes jutted out from the logs, and some of them had the skulls of humans, dwarves, elves, and orcs on them. Enemies who entered the cave would be crushed and impaled by the walls of logs, which would fall from both sides at the same time and block the tunnel leading deeper into the lair.

Ukluk hopped over the shallow—but wide—crack in the middle of the entry cave where he was forced to sleep. If they were attacked, he would sound the alarm horn and trigger the log trap if the guards failed to do so. Since Ukluk had given Kar-Pok the idea and helped build the trap, the little orc had made certain there were no spikes that would hit him while he hid in the streambed-like depression that ran along the floor in case he was there when the trap was sprung.

He ran into the chief's sleeping cave deeper inside and lifted the totem of the tribe. The long metal spear— with a rusty tip—was actually a solid iron spike over seven feet long, and had been in the possession of the tribe for many orc lifetimes. According to Kar-Pok, it had been used by the infamous Horde King Grashcar, who had impaled hundreds of elves and humans, as well as all of the orc chieftains who would not follow him and the once-vast Iron Spear tribe into the battle that had become known by all races as 'The Breaking.' Tens of thousands of orcs had been annihilated by a combined force of elves and men on the plains of Beykla. The remnants of the Iron Spear tribe were among the smattering of Drunda's spawn that remained in Beykla, while the rest fled south.

Ukluk hefted the spear, likely of dwarf manufacture—though he would never mention that to any of the tribe unless he wanted to be impaled on it himself. He carried it out of the lair as fast as he could, trying not to bang either end of it on the walls. Once outside the spear was ripped from his hands by howling warriors. Two of the whelps left the drums to beat him with their clubs, playing his skull like a drum instead. Ukluk protected his eyes and crawled away from his attackers as Kar-Pok put a human skull on the tip of the spear and raised it over his head. The drumming and howling soon reached a frenzy.

"Drunda, Drunda, Drunda!" the orcs chanted as they beat their drums.

Kar-Pok suddenly brought the spear down and crushed the skull on top of it against a rock, causing many excited hoots. He shouted to the warriors, handed the spear to Kar-Vrishnek who would keep it safe, and then Kar-Pok charged into night.

"Kar-Pok!" The warriors shouted as they ran after the chief.

As the odor and the sound of the war party faded, Ukluk breathed a sigh of relief. If his plan worked, this would be the last time he ever saw Kar-Pok and the others. He spoke silently to the Angry God as Valga had taught him. *Cruel Drunda, accept the blood offering Ukluk makes in anger. Kill these orcs and accept their blood.*

Moonlight glinted off an axe-blade that fell toward Ukluk's head. He tried to duck out of the way, but the flat of an axe glanced across his thick skull and knocked him over. He barely felt the blow, thanks to his inch-thick skull, quick reflexes and the fact that the blow was only meant to get his attention.

"Slave,"–Kar-Vrishnek pointed at him with his axe—"No-Tusks mine now."

Ukluk groveled, pressing his snout into the dirt. "Kar-Vrishnek's slave."

"Get us some bog wine and tell the females to lock up the milk suckers. We're coming for a visit." Meglarg grunted his approval and snapped his teeth together, all the while keeping a hold on Feglak, who was still trying to follow the war party.

Vrishnek flicked Feglak on the forehead where Ukluk had put the metal plate. The large orc apparently forgot what he was doing and stopped trying to run after the war party. Feglak looked at Vrishnek like it was the first time he had ever seen him.

Back inside the lair, Ukluk served the three wounded warriors chunky bog wine served in bronze helmets sized for human skulls. The smell of rotting blood—kept from clotting with willow bark and other plants—mixed with pregnant orc urine, and as many types of fermenting grapes, radishes, berries, and onions as could be found, made Ukluk wish he had just taken a bigger drink from the jug before he mixed in a secret ingredient.

Vrishnek and his comrades drained their large cups and howled for more.

"Bring a file-stone and more bog wine," Vrishnek commanded.

Ukluk shuddered and instinctively hid the nubs of his tusks with his lips. Kar-Pok hadn't filed them in a while—they were starting to grow back. Instead of bringing what had been asked for, Ukluk hid outside the cave and waited. The three orcs soon became silent and snores replaced the sound of their harsh voices. The sleeping mushrooms worked even faster than he had anticipated, probably because he'd gathered them earlier that day.

Satisfied, Ukluk went into the hills beside the lair and retrieved the gifts he would give to Imyak and her two sisters. The trembling calf was still lashed to the tree, its mouth tied shut so it could make little noise. Using the small cow as a pack animal, Ukluk loaded it with the two sealed pots of honey he had collected and led the animal toward the lair. The calf refused to enter the pitch-black cave and Ukluk reasoned that the darkness and the odor wafting out of the entrance must have frightened it.

The clip-clop of its hooves would alert the whelps inside, so Ukluk picked it up, carrying the baby cow on his shoulders, dangling its legs around his neck. Now all he had to do was get past the whelps. Much deeper inside the hill he could hear them banging on drums and fighting. One yelled, "Chief of Pit!" Roars and howls echoed as the other young orcs challenged for dominance and attacked en masse.

The entrance to the females' cave was within sight when something wet and slimy struck Ukluk in the middle of his back. Another piece of filth hit him in the face when he turned around.

Three whelps, none more than four winters old, stood behind him scowling with mad hunger in their eyes.

"Give food." The strongest of the whelps said, eying the calf. He was almost the same size as Ukluk, but was thinner and weaker. These three had likely decided to avoid the game in the pit, as they had no chance of winning, and a greater chance of being maimed or killed.

"No. Not for you." Ukluk stepped backward slowly, trying not to provoke the young ones.

"Give now!"

"Mine!"

"Food!"

The tallest whelp threw a rock that hit Ukluk's crotch. He was used to being struck in his scaly bollocks, and had developed a tolerance over the years that allowed him to shrug off the pain. He turned to run, and without any warning his legs were knocked out from under him by an emaciated two-winter-old whelp that had been hiding in a garbage-filled niche. The three whelps behind him were on Ukluk in an instant trying to tear the calf from his arms. Ukluk maintained a death-grip on the animal as one of the young orcs managed to pull the binding from the calf's mouth. The squirming animal mooed in terror. The youngest whelp began gnawing on one of the calf's legs as Ukluk got to his feet and began tugging the calf down the tunnel, dragging the little whelps with him.

The sounds of fighting in the pit stopped.

All of the orcs froze, as did the struggling calf.

"Bad. Much bad," Ukluk said, as the urine in his bladder felt like it had turned to ice.

Nearly a dozen bloodied and bruised whelps emerged from the pit at the end of the tunnel like demons from the Abyss. The odor of sulfur-tinged sweat and bloodied orclings wafted down the hall.

"Food!" Kapik, the largest whelp, who was likely Kar-Pok's son, shouted as he led the charge at Ukluk. The smaller whelps climbed up the walls or slipped into cracks in the rock.

The frightened slave orc ran for the females' cave as fast as he could, pulling the calf along with him. He slammed into the thorn-bush-and-log barrier that was strong enough to keep the whelps out, but not strong enough to keep the adult orcs from paying visits to Imyak and her two sisters whenever they wanted.

"Imyak! No-Tusks has food!" Ukluk shouted as he banged on the barricade.

Grabbing claws and hungry mouths attached themselves to the calf as the orclings yanked Ukluk to the ground. He tried to defend himself, but there were too many.

The log barrier came down and a squat orc female with pendulous breasts, a large swollen belly, and hateful eyes, leapt into the passageway with a flat club in one fist and a three-pronged whip in the other.

"Flee!" The whelps squealed with dread as Imyak, the Spawn Mother of Iron Spear tribe unleashed her fury, beating the orclings mercilessly and whipping them as they ran away. When she finished paddling Kapik, whom she had caught with her whip, she picked him up by his scraggly hair and tossed him down the tunnel.

"Stay in pit!" Imyak shouted at her son.

Ukluk crawled into the females' cave, following the calf who had already gone inside. Imyak closed the barricade and grinned at the bruised slave orc, who knelt at her feet.

"No-Tusks brings food," Imyak said to her two smaller sisters. Ugash, and Oogrook came out of the shadows from the smaller grotto where all their milk suckers were caged. If left to crawl around the lair, the little biters would fall into crevasses and die or be killed by their older siblings.

Ugash and Oogrook's bellies were as swollen as Imyak's, and soon they would spawn a new brood— like they did every seven months. If the spawning went well, Imyak, Ugash, and Oogrook would survive the ordeal. Up to nine, but at least six new whelps would be born. Too many of the Iron Spear females had died in mating or birth accidents over the past few seasons. The tribe was getting smaller as female whelps were rarely born. Not even two in five births yielded a female, and only a few survived to adulthood because of their harsh treatment. The way the Iron Spear males treated the females made Ukluk angry. Females were rare, and he would never treat them so badly if he had power. Unless they deserved it, no more females would die violently if Ukluk's plans came to pass.

The little orc's desire grew as he inhaled the

intoxicating odor of the three sisters and their cave, where the tribe's stores of meat—some salted, some rotting—were kept. Then he presented the calf to them. Imyak licked her lips and the younger sisters rubbed their bulbous stomachs. "I bring more." Ukluk unloaded the two small honey pots from the trembling calf, relieved the stout ceramic jars had not broken in the scuffle outside. "Now No-Tusks make favorite food of Imyak and sisters."

The slave orc used a rock to crush the calf's skull, then he hung the body on a rope and slit its throat. He dripped a large amount of blood into each honey pot, much to the delight of the sisters. Ugash gave him a large urn to drain the rest of the blood as he mixed the honey, then presented the pots to them

"Fresh blood honey is best," Imyak said as she dipped her fingers into the pot and slurped the red, sticky substance off her fingers. "No-Tusks good. Only orc who brings blood honey."

None of the warriors were smart enough to get the honey without suffering many stings on their vulnerable ears, snout, and lips. Ukluk's exceptional climbing skills allowed him to go where the larger and heavier orcs would never dare. They used him as their honey-gatherer, sometimes forcing him to retrieve the honey after they had already infuriated the bees.

Imyak patted Ukluk on the head and gently smeared some of her mucus on his wounded ear. The females valued him now, a stark difference compared to the first time he tried to mate with them. Several of the warriors had just had their way with the sisters and Ukluk thought he might have a chance. It was the worst mistake he had ever made since joining the tribe and losing his tusks. Imyak, Ugash, and Oogrook pummeled him for so long that it took a month before he could see out of his left eye again. He thought he would never mate with a female until he saw the longing in Imyak's eyes when Kar-Pok feasted on a jar of blood honey. Then he knew how to win them over.

The females ate the blood honey and nibbled on small bits of raw veal as Ukluk butchered the animal for them. He presented the warm liver to Imyak. She slurped a piece of it into her mouth and chewed, allowing some of the blood to drip onto her alluring boil-marked chin and down her chest.

"Come, No-Tusks." Imyak invited him to clean the drippings from her body as she lay down on her back, offering the reward he most desired. He enjoyed the taste of the blood as he lay with Imyak quenching his lust. It had taken him a long time, but Ukluk had found a way to mate with the females. He didn't need to bite their necks with his tusks and hold them down.

Near dawn, Ukluk asked Imyak to remove the heavy barricade so he could go to his sleeping place in the entry cave. No one had been guarding the lair entrance, though he doubted that anyone would break through the wooden gate without the whelps calling an alarm.

Imyak grabbed his arm as he got up to depart, and touched his hand to her belly. "Imyak and sisters spawn soon." Ukluk felt the writhing whelps, punching and wrestling inside her body. Her abdomen was much smaller than usual when she was about to birth whelps, and that made Ukluk proud. He had given the females' orc-seed-killing tea and the sisters had used it after every encounter with the gangs of Iron Spear orcs who visited them. They did not drink it after he lay with them and in perhaps a week his first whelps would be born. Their smaller birth-size would make it less likely that Imyak or the others would die during the whelping process.

There was so much to do before that exciting day. He sneaked past the whelp pit and into the cave where Vrishnek, Feglak, and Meglarg were sleeping. He prayed to Drunda that the poison mushrooms he'd given them would keep them asleep as he completed his task. Using a club and his sharp claws he bruised and scratched the three orcs, mimicking the injuries they would have suffered if they had mated with the females. None of the warriors awakened, despite the beating he gave them. Ukluk considered killing them, but murdering the three orcs with his own hand was not in his plans. Their deaths would be much more painful.

"*Garga!*" Kar-Vrishnek shouted, the echoing word waking Ukluk from his blissful slumber. The slave orc pressed himself into the floor a moment later in front of the angry Kar. The sun had just set and the lair had come alive with howling and banging. Imyak and her sisters were feeding the whelps chunks of rotting meat.

The young orcs jostled to see who would be first.

"Slave, what happened last night?" Kar-Vrishnek inspected the scratch marks on his arms. Meglarg and Feglak were still passed out and snoring loudly.

"Kar drink much bog wine," Ukluk said. "Much time with females. They fight hard."

Kar-Vrishnek rubbed his other scratches, wiped his crotch, and then smelled his fingers. "Kar-Vrishnek not smell females."

Ukluk hid his fear as well as he could. What should he say to this? He stammered, "Kar smells like bog wine."

Vrishnek grabbed Ukluk, pinned him to the ground by sitting on him and inspected the nubs of his growing tusks. "Kar-Vrishnek not remember filing slave's tusks last night. Kar-Vrishnek do it now."

The abrasive stone caused shooting pains every time Vrishnek scraped it across Ukluk's sensitive tusk buds. As he endured the agonizing humiliation he tried to think about Imyak and the taste of calf liver on her leathery skin.

The next day Ukluk tossed and turned in the shallow crack where he slept in the entry cave. His tusk buds throbbed painfully as he prayed to Drunda and asked the Angry God to make today the day that his new ally would arrive and punish Kar-Vrishnek. He pulled his stiff deer-hide blanket over his face as the bright morning light beamed into the lair and bothered his eyes. At least Kar-Pok and the war party hadn't returned. Ukluk allowed himself to hope that all of them had been slain in the trap he'd sent them into. If only the next part of his plan would come to pass. To ease his mind, he chewed on a dried lizard tail and eventually fell back asleep as the light faded.

"Halloo!"

The deep echoing voice blasted into the cave like rolling thunder. Ukluk shot awake, and scrambled to the guard post, fear tempering his excitement as he pressed against the wooden bars of the gate.

"Halloo! I smell orcs in there!"

Kar-Vrishnek, Feglak, and eventually limping Meglarg arrived a moment later. They picked up weapons and shields as they hid behind the gate.

"What words he say?" Kar-Vrishnek asked.

"Sound like man words," Meglarg said.

"It's a giant's words," Ukluk said. "Giants speak words like the men of Beykla."

"Slave understands man words?" Vrishnek asked.

Ukluk nodded. "No-Tusks understands." The words of men had been the secret way that Valga the witch had spoken to him when she did not want the chief to know what she said. Knowing the man words had allowed Ukluk to slowly become the giant's servant and ally.

"Can giant get into Iron Spear lair?" Meglarg asked, trying to balance on his one good leg.

"No. Too big," Ukluk said.

"Ask giant what giant wants," Kar-Vrishnek said.

"Giant, why are you here?" Ukluk asked in his best man-speech.

"That you, No-Tusks? You know why."

"No-Tusks knows. But guard chief of lair wants No-Tusks to ask because Mungo has come when war chief who sent me to speak to Mungo is not is not in lair."

Mungo made an irritated noise. "No-Tusks, tell your stupid guard chief that I, Mungo the Red, am here because your chief asked me to come. Now I will lead your tribe on raids. I am the new war chief. Tell them that if all the orcs in this tribe do not follow me, I'll bury this cave and no orc will ever get out alive."

Ukluk made his face contort with fear. His eyes bulged, his knees wavered, and he let a squirt of urine run down his leg. It was the performance he had been practicing for his entire life.

"What giant say?" Vrishnek asked, a tremble in his voice.

"Giant say giant is Mungo the Bloody Haired, new chief of Iron Spear tribe. Giant say that if we not follow him, giant will pour oil into cave, smoke us out, or burn us to death. If tribe go out the escape-holes he will hunt us, peel our skin, and eat all orcs while still alive."

"Iron Spear tribe fights!" Feglak said, weakly raising his hammer.

"No." Vrishnek pulled down the weapon. "Mungo the Bloody Haired will kill us. We need more warriors to fight giant. No-Tusks, tell giant that tribe surrenders."

"Tribe surrenders?" Ukluk asked with a grave expression, hiding his joy.

Vrishnek pushed the slave hard into the entry cave. "Tell him, now."

Ukluk faced the entrance to the lair. "Chief Mungo, the orcs of this tribe who want to serve you are away on a raid," Ukluk said. "There are only three warriors here and they will not serve a smelly red haired man-giant who has relations with small goats. They hate your kind, and want to put the totem spear of tribe into your arse and hammer it until it pokes out of your mouth."

Mungo roared angrily. "You tell those dung eating orcs that I will crush their skulls with my bare hands."

Ukluk cringed, reasoning that it would take quite a while even for a giant to crush an orc's skull. He would definitely like to see Vrishnek's skull crushed.

"What giant say?" Vrishnek asked.

"Giant say he accepts surrender of Iron Spear tribe, and wants warriors to march outside, raise weapons to sky, and shout Mungo's name in man words to show we surrender."

"What his man name?" Vrishnek asked.

"*We kill Mungo,*" Ukluk said in man words.

Kar-Vrishnek and Meglarg repeated the words, though it took them a couple of tries to get them right. Feglak looked at them stupidly, not understanding what was happening.

"Tell him we are coming out," Vrishnek said.

"The orcs who hate you are coming out to fight," Ukluk said. "They will try to kill you, but they are very frightened."

"Let them come." Mungo said, then laughed heartily.

"He is pleased that you are surrendering," Ukluk said.

Kar-Vrishnek grunted his approval as the three orc warriors of the Iron Spear tribe emerged from their lair, shielding their eyes from the sun, which had luckily gone behind a cloud. Meglarg used his axe as a crutch to hobble out, Vrishnek held his axe with his one good arm and Feglak had a wild pre-battle look in his eyes as he squeezed the handle of his heavy war hammer. Ukluk shuffled behind them, grinning devilishly on the inside, but trembling on the outside.

Twelve-foot-tall Mungo the Red stood several paces away from the entrance. He wore grizzly bear pelts over his pale skin, which was covered with freckles and dirt. His beard and hair were orange-red and he carried a large knotted club made from a black oak tree.

The three orcs stood warily before the giant, the sun partially blinding them. Vrishnek nodded to Meglarg, giving him the signal. "We kill Mungo!" The orcs shouted in man words as they raised their weapons.

Mungo raised his club and crushed Vrishnek's skull. The orc's body crumpled like his bones had turned to swamp jelly.

Meglarg squealed and tried to flee back into the cave. Feglak screamed his battle cry and charged Mungo. The amused giant grabbed the attacking orc by the head with one massive hand, stopping him cold. Ukluk 'accidentally fell' in front of Meglarg and tripped the fleeing orc, giving Mungo enough time to bash the one-legged warrior in the other leg, then in the spine—killing him instantly.

Feglak clawed at Mungo's thick wrist. The giant picked up the orc by the head, broke both his arms with blows from his club, then put Feglak's head into his hairy red armpit and squeezed, grunting like he was trying to pass nightsoil that had been hardening for a week. After quite a long time, Mungo's face turned red with effort, then Feglak's skull imploded. Even after gray goo and blood ran onto the ground, the orc's body quivered.

"No-Tusks," Mungo said at last, pointing at Ukluk. "You are my slave now. You will speak to the tribe for me."

"No-Tusks is slave of Chief Mungo." Ukluk bowed, relieved the giant had kept to their bargain. The story was that Ukluk would become Mungo's personal slave as a gift from Chief Kar-Pok. Mungo would become the war chief of the tribe and the orcs would be able to hunt in Mungo's territory.

"Slave, go and fetch me fresh meat and drink."

"Fresh meat we have, Chief Mungo, but for drinking we have brown water and bog wine. Brown water not good and only orcs like bog wine."

Mungo shook his head. "My people taught orcs how to make bog wine. Bring it now."

Ukluk knew what food Mungo hungered for, and had a smirk on his face when he entered the lair cave. He found the whelps huddled together in their pit. Some of the smaller ones perched in ledges on the walls. All of them looked at Ukluk with fear for the first time ever.

Imyak and her sisters stood beside the pit with spears in hand. Mismatched pieces of rusty armor covered their teats and pregnant bellies.

Ukluk put his hands on his hips. "Vrishnek, Meglarg and Feglak are meat."

The whelps shuddered and the younger ones squealed.

"Mungo the Bloody Haired giant is new chief of Iron Spear tribe."

The sound of urine hitting the floor pleased Ukluk very much.

"Chief Mungo wants all orclings to become his new warriors. He wants to see how strong you fight. He will take the strongest as his raiding party."

"No, we hide in cave!" Kapik, Kar-Pok's son shouted. He was the tallest, meanest, and apparently the most intelligent of all the whelps.

Imyak's whip cracked against the stone. "Iron Spear tribe fights. No hiding. Go serve Chief Mungo."

"No." Kapik stood defiantly, his snout raised, a snarl on his lips.

Imyak jumped into the pit and latched her hands around Kapik's throat. She throttled him and smashed him against the side of the pit, then threw him by the scruff of the neck. "Go fight for new chief."

All of the whelps followed as Kapik staggered out of the lair. They shuddered when they saw the bodies of the three adult orcs. Fourteen whelps, aged from two- to eight-winters presented themselves to Mungo, who leaned against the hill beside the entrance of the lair. The orclings carried jugs of bog wine that Ukluk had secretly spiked with special ingredients—every last bit of his strongest poisons. The giant smirked at the orclings as they shielded their eyes from the sunlight.

"This all?" Mungo asked.

"Only teat suckers and females left in cave," Ukluk said.

"Small tribe." Mungo shook his head. "What happened? Disease? Elves? Infighting?"

Ukluk grunted. "All things Chief Mungo say have made tribe small, and too much inbreeding make tribe weak." The slave handed the giant a jug of bog wine.

"Chief Mungo, whelps want to show how strong they are. They will fight each other. Winner will be spared. Losers are first to be fresh meat in chief's belly."

Mungo took a draught from the jug, spilling some of the bloody liquor onto his beard. "Strong," he said through puckered lips. "Who made this?"

"No-Tusks make bog wine," the slave said.

"Good. You will stay close by Mungo. I will keep you safe for a long time, and you will make bog wine for me in my cave." The giant grabbed Ukluk and deftly fastened a chain around his neck, the other end of which was attached to a metal loop around his belt.

This was not part of Ukluk's plan, and if he was tied to the giant how would he survive what was to come? Ukluk kept his sphincters tight. He could show no fear now.

"Make them fight," Mungo ordered Ukluk. "I am hungry."

It didn't take long for Ukluk to get the whelps to begin their blood matches. They did this every night in their pit, and enjoyed trying to kill and maim each other with bare fists and tusks. A pair of two-winter-old whelps went first and neither had learned that punches to the head were ineffective. Finally, one choked the other out and stood in triumph, howling and stomping on his fallen cousin. Mungo picked up the fallen whelp, whom he proceeded to tear apart and eat raw.

The subsequent matches became more and more vicious as the whelps realized the giant would eat the losers. The younger whelps fell to the older ones. Mungo filled his belly with the most tender meaty parts of half a dozen little orclings before his gut bulged past his belt. To the relief of the whelps, the giant stopped eating after half the matches were fought, instead drinking more and more bog wine. Ukluk waited nervously, then noticed Mungo rubbing his stomach and looking quite ill. His face was pale, his lips slightly blue. The poison was beginning to work, and if the giant realized what was happening while Ukluk was chained to him, the little slave orc would be killed long before Mungo succumbed to the poison.

"I've eaten too much orc flesh," Mungo said.

"Chief, let No-Tusks help." Ukluk began forming a plan as Mungo pulled the chain, lightly choking him.

"How will you help me?"

"Chalk stone in lair. If you eat chalk stone, you be well."

"Get it while I watch the rest of the fights."

Kapik finished pummeling one of his brothers and stood victorious, eying Ukluk suspiciously.

"Chief take chain off No-Tusks?"

Mungo shook his head and took another chain from a pouch and used it to lengthen the chain around Ukluk's neck. "This is as far as you go."

The chain was longer than Ukluk thought and it reached just past the midway point of the entry cave. He called for Imyak and she appeared instantly, as she had been hiding at the guard post. Her eyes focused on the chain. "Imyak fetch hammer and pry bar for No-Tusks."

"No, bring totem iron spear," Ukluk said.

"Slave!" Mungo shouted. "Bring the chalk!" The chain jerked and Ukluk was pulled off his feet, his air cut off as he was dragged across the floor. He was going to die when he was so close to getting what he wanted. Right before he passed out the chain went slack. Ukluk gasped for breath, trying to recover his senses.

Imyak appeared, a determined expression on her boil-marked face as she carried the iron spear along with a sack containing a hammer, chisel, and pry bar. He crawled toward her and slipped the ring of iron that kept him collared over the spear shaft and down to the halfway point of its length. "Push spear into hole in stone." Ukluk pointed to an opening in the depression in the floor where he had slept for the past three years. He had drilled it himself to drain rainwater and other fluids that tended to be deposited where he slept.

Imyak drove the shaft downward. Three feet of the iron spear disappeared in the rock. The shaft would move side to side, but would not budge if pulled toward the cave mouth. Ukluk positioned himself behind it, setting his feet in place, and desperately hoping that

Mungo would not be able to break the spear or pry it loose. "Imyak, wait at guard place." She obeyed immediately, and Ukluk felt a strange emotion for Imyak that he never had before. He did not know what longing feeling was, but it was much stronger than the primal lust he usually had when he smelled her.

"Slave? Come. Now!" Mungo slurred his words as the poison took hold. "What are you doing? Hurry." The giant pulled on the chain, but the shaft held fast.

Ukluk kept silent, refusing to answer the dying giant. Finally, after some loud shouting and jerking on the chain the giant peered warily into the cavern.

"Slave, you defy your chief?" Mungo pulled on the chain hard and Ukluk noticed the ring binding him start to come open, the metal bending. He was almost free.

Mungo noticed it too and stopped pulling. "You are smart for a slave orc. Come here and I shall kill you quickly."

"No-Tusks stays. I wait and watch Mungo die."

Mungo's face scrunched up. He coughed, clutching his abdomen, the horror on his face turning to rage as he realized he had been poisoned.

Ukluk shook his head and said, "No-Tusks tell Mungo not to drink the bog wine."

The giant roared and the whelps outside started squealing in panic. Mungo vented his rage on them, and Ukluk heard several of the orclings die from the giant's blows as the rest fled into the hills. Mungo returned a moment later with blood and gore on his hands. Ukluk recoiled as the giant reached into the cave. "I'll break your bones then peel off your hide." Mungo squeezed his head and shoulders through the opening of the cave, his hand coming closer.

Ukluk shouted, "Imyak, now!"

The female pulled the lever. The spiked log walls did not fall on the giant. They remained in place, the empty eye sockets on the elf and dwarf skulls mocking Ukluk.

Mungo grinned as he came closer and reached for the little orc.

Ukluk's eyes bulged.

Imyak kicked part of the log wall trap and heavy timbers fell on the giant. Metal spikes pierced Mungo's body and crushed him to the ground. Ukluk flattened himself inside the crack in the floor as the iron spear was pushed over. When the dust began to settle, Mungo moaned in pain, trapped under the logs.

Safe in his sleeping place, Ukluk used the hammer, chisel, and pry bar to free himself from the chain, wedging apart one of the links. He crawled along the crack to the edge of the cave and slipped out the escape-hole that led deeper into the lair. He wanted to see Imyak, but there would be time for that later. Ukluk slipped out of the lair using one of the secret tunnels and found himself looking down on the legs of the dying giant. Would the poison in the bog wine kill him, or would blood loss from the spiked logs? He didn't know for sure, and thought Mungo would have been long dead by now from the poisons. At least Mungo had slain all but two or three whelps. Kapik's body was not among the ones outside, and that made

Ukluk nervous.

Dropping rocks on the giant's back bone took up the rest of the afternoon, and by evening there were few stones left that Ukluk could move by himself. He would have to recruit Imyak and her sisters.

Movement in the bushes at the edge of the clearing in front of the lair made Ukluk hide on his belly. Fear made his heart skip several beats as a group of three adult orcs emerged from the shadows. *Drunda's bollacks!* Ukluk cursed silently, some of the war party had survived. The orcs stared at the giant's legs poking out of their lair long enough to raise their weapons, then charged, screaming for blood. The first one to hit the giant cut his leg open with a vicious overhand axe chop. Mungo's leg jerked and struck the orc under the chin and snapped his head back with enough force to kill him instantly.

Enraged, Kar-Pok leapt onto the giant's back and chopped at Mungo's back until he stopped moving. Torgash, the lone surviving orc warrior, climbed up and stood with his chief upon Mungo's paralyzed body. The whelp, Kapik, appeared at the edge of the clearing and howled victoriously, shouting his father's name.

Ukluk thought about slinking off into the night, never to return. He started to slip away and his foot dislodged a pebble, which rolled down the hill.

Kapik rushed forward pointing at Ukluk and grunting.

Kar-Pok backed up from the giant and spotted Ukluk. "Come here, slave."

Ukluk's bones turned to swamp slime. He could never outrun them. Instead, Ukluk crawled down the hill and prostrated himself at Kar-Pok's feet. The war leader kicked him in the side. "What happened?"

"Giant killed warriors and many whelps," Ukluk said.

"Why did tribe come out of lair?" Kar-Pok asked.

"Slave made bad things happen," Kapik said.

"No," Ukluk said, "Kar-Vrishnek and the warriors were meat. No-Tusks saved tribe. No-Tusks poison giant with bog wine, then drop the logs on him. No-Tusks save tribe."

Kapik opened his jaws to speak, but his father cut him off with a backhanded slap. "Kapik ran into the woods," Kar-Pok accused his son, then threw him to the ground. "Kapik is frightened dog while slave stay, fight as warrior."

"Good slave," Ukluk groveled in the dirt, eying Kapik with contempt.

Kar-Pok shook his head at Kapik. "Kar-Pok lets coward whelp live for now. Coward will help butcher giant so tribe has meat until next moon."

"Other warriors not coming with cattle?" Ukluk asked, a glimmer of hope returning.

"No." Kar-Pok said, shaking his head grimly. "Warriors ambushed on way to raid."

Ukluk tried to look as surprised as he could, though he wanted to play the elf-skin drums and chant Drunda's name. The Angry God had accepted most of his offering, but why had Drunda not taken Kar-Pok and Torgash?

"No matter that cattle not taken. Tribe has many things to eat now," Kar-Pok said, as he glanced at the giant, the warriors, and the dead whelps strewn about. "Harvest this meat. Waste nothing."

Three days later, Ukluk lay in his sleeping place in entry cave, staring up at the dried blood on the spikes on the reset log trap. His sense of dread increased with every howl of pain echoing from the females' cave deeper in the lair. He should go now, flee while Kar-Pok and Torgash were distracted by the bloody spectacle in the birth cave. Ukluk would lose himself in the swamp tonight, then make his way to Mungo's lair where they had made their agreement. Perhaps someday Ukluk would find another tribe and join them. He would start over. As a slave. Again.

Imyak and her sisters would face the wrath of Kar-Pok alone. They would probably survive the terrible punishment, but if he stayed, Ukluk would not. The screaming in the birth cave increased in volume, three voices howling as they dropped their whelps, one after another as the little biters charged out of their mothers. Oogrook's voice was the loudest. Of the three sisters she was the most affected by pain, and required the most milk of the poppy after giving birth. He should have prepared some for her in advance.

Head hanging down, Ukluk gathered his meager belongings into a sack, put his poisoned needles into a sheath on his wrist, and prepared to leave the lair of the

Iron Spear tribe forever.

The howling stopped. It could only mean one thing. All of the whelps had come. Ukluk's whelps, though he would never see them. If only Kar-Pok had been killed in the ambush, everything would have been different. Perhaps if he had had more time, Ukluk could gather some poison mushrooms from the swamp and take care of the chief and Torgash.

Harsh shouting echoed from the depths. An enraged Kar-Pok spewed curses at the females. Imyak's voice pleaded and a brood of newborn orclings began to wail. Oogrook or Ugash—definitely not Imyak—screamed for mercy as Ukluk nearly went mad with worry. Would the chief kill the females and all the newborn milk suckers? How could Ukluk let this happen?

"Kar-Pok!" Ukluk screamed as loud as he could, his challenge filled with hatred. The chief's name reverberated off the walls. It could not be taken back or mistaken for what it was. Ukluk would not run. Not today.

The little slave wrapped the pull-cord for the log trap he had installed around his ankle and waited. He thought about the poison needles hidden in his wrist sheath, but knew the poison was not strong enough to kill orcs as strong as Kar-Pok or Torgash.

The stomping sounds of the chief and Torgash coming to kill Ukluk were unmistakable. The pair of rage-filled orcs burst into the entry cave and Kar-Pok dangled a mewling newborn whelp by a skinny green leg.

Veins in Kar-Pok's forehead bulged as he glared at

the tiny orcling, so obviously slave spawn. "No-Tusks put slave seed in all females. No-Tusks gets prisoner treatment, then Kar-Pok finishes slave by heating up totem iron spear and impaling slave on red hot metal."

Torgash laughed, then said, "We make No-Tusks tell how he force females to mate with slave."

Ukluk shrugged. "I tell how."

The two warriors paused and Ukluk said, "Females do anything for blood honey."

Ukluk thought he saw both Kar-Pok and Torgash nodding their heads at the moment he jerked the pull-cord with his ankle, fell prone, and triggered the spiked logs, which fell and killed the surprised orcs.

Lying safe in the fissure where he slept, Ukluk listened for the sound of the newborn Kar-Pok had been holding. There was nothing. He sighed remorsefully, knowing Imyak and her sisters had probably had sets of twins at least, if not triplets. He had to find out. He crawled though the fissure to the escape-tunnel, which led deeper into the lair.

He crawled to the edge of the cavern and went down the escape-hole. He had to see Imyak and his brood of newborn whelps. The strange feeling returned when he thought of Imyak. He realized that he coveted her more than anything else. She would be his, and his alone. No other male would ever have her again, and if they did, Ukluk would kill them.

Something hard cracked him on the back of the neck as he emerged from the narrow tunnel. Ukluk crumpled to the ground as the young orc Kapik stood over him, brandishing an iron-shod club.

"No-Tusks be Kar-Kapik's slave now," the whelp said, then struck Ukluk on the snout. Kar-Kapik beat Ukluk with the war club, striking his legs, arms, feet, and head.

Bloody and dazed, Ukluk groveled on the floor and licked Kar-Kapik's feet. "Good slave. No-Tusks is Kar-Kapik's slave now."

The whelp grunted after sudden pain, kicked Ukluk in the face, and stumbled backwards. Kar-Kapik fell to the ground and held his foot, inspecting the trickle of blood coming from his ankle. "What No-Tusks do?"

Ukluk showed the dying whelp the metal needle he had stabbed him with and swallowed the delicious blood in his mouth. "No-Tusks kills Kar-Kapik."

The whelp slumped to the floor, his muscles twitching. Ukluk crawled on top of Kapik and sat on his chest.

"No-Tusks never be warrior, never be Kar, never be chief," Kapik said as tremors wracked his entire body.

Ukluk nodded. "No-Tusks never be called chief, but No-Tusks is only father of new tribe. When these grow long, tribe will call me Tezok the Witch Doctor."

"Warriors will kill No-Tusks," Kapik said, his tongue swelling in his mouth.

Ukluk snarled, displaying his newly filed tusks and hungering for the day when they would grow back and he could reclaim his old name.

"No-Tusks"–the whelp gagged—"is nothing."

"Not nothing. No orc will cross Witch Doctor Poison Master of Drunda."

Kapik's eyes bulged as he died choking on his own tongue.

Satisfied, Ukluk strolled down the empty tunnel eager to see Imyak, Ugash, Oogrook, and his spawn. He would make many more orclings with the females until the entire tribe was just like him: short, clever, and ruthless. The Angry God Drunda had accepted the blood of all the Iron Spear tribes' warriors, some of its whelps, and most importantly, a red haired giant had been defeated by him.

The omens were clear.

The new tribe would prosper, and someday, Ukluk—no, Tezok!—would send his sons on raids with Drunda's poison on their weapons. Humans and elves would fear the Poisoned Spear tribe above all others. *It will all come to pass*, he thought, as he rubbed the nubs of his tusks, knowing that they would never be filed down again.

Watch a not-safe-for-work video of author Paul Genesse and Patrick M. Tracy reading from "No-Tusks" here: vimeo.com/24400613

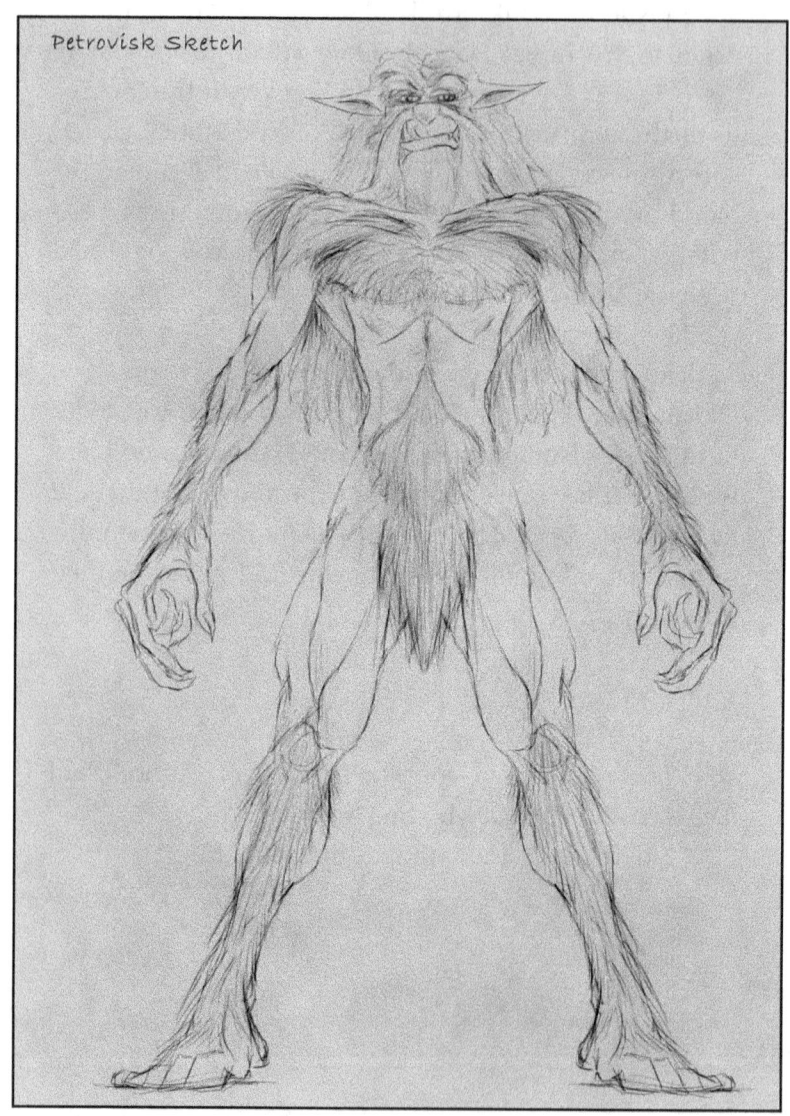

"Petrovisk" by Kendall R. Hart

A Kudekah to Remember
by Paul Genesse and Shane Moore

"You bring much shame to the greyshalks."

Petrovisk lowered his head to hide the humiliation in his yellow eyes as he knelt inside the smoky tent.

His angry father, a full head taller when they were standing side by side, towered over him. "Seven failed kudekahs. You return with nothing to make the clan stronger, nothing for the cook-fires or for the totem tree. The ancestor spirits have abandoned you. That is why you cannot hunt. Greyshalks who do not bring home meat are good for nothing."

The young greyshalk did not want to believe, but his father, Grawlin, was a clan elder and a powerful shaman who had walked to all corners of the greyshalk lands. Grawlin spoke with the animal spirits and the long dead ancestors from the first greyshalk clan. If he said the spirits had turned away from Petrovisk, it was true. He had failed to complete his rite of passage from pup to kip more times than any other who had not been banished. The memory songs said he should not be allowed to stay, even if he was born from a mate of a clan elder as respected as his father.

Grawlin tugged on the long tufts of grey fur

dangling from his chin. "You will not disgrace our family for any more sunrises. The ancestor songs say you have until the next full moon, but the spirits have spoken. You will walk away from the camp and never come back. You will not be a shaman of the clan when I have gone."

"Please, Father, let me try again."

"No. You will banish yourself before the elders send you away and shame me in front of the entire clan."

His father was right. If he failed another kudekah he would bring even more disgrace to his family. Everyone knew how many times he had tried and failed. So many failures might even cause the spirits to leave all the clans hunters and the greyshalks would starve. All because of him.

Grawlin sighed. "This clan must never smell, hear or see you again. If we do, your blood will be shed. Go from these lands. You are banished for all the sunrises and sunsets of your life. Your name will never be heard in the memory songs."

Petrovisk's shoulders slumped. Not having his name in the songs was a terrible punishment. He would not be with his people in this world or the next. He would not be part of creating the new songs as a shaman, and he had spent his entire life memorizing all of the songs. He knew every one, and some said he knew them better than the elders, better than his own father, who ignored some of the oldest songs when the elders' new ways were against the traditions of the past.

He ducked out through the tent flap. The chill

winter wind cut through the hair on his arms and legs. He wanted to go to the fire at the center of the camp of animal hide tents where most of the clan had gathered. Freshly killed elk and deer roasted over the fire, and the smell made his stomach rumble. Young pups played and laughed, and he saw Alenka sitting on a log, a bearskin blanket around her shoulders. Would this be the last time he saw her?

He wanted Alenka to turn and look at him, but then she would know he was a failure, and he would see the sadness in her eyes. Better to remember her in a different way, and she must forget about him.

Petrovisk put on his skikkja, the fur cloak Alenka had made for him when winter began. He picked up his flint-tipped spear and his nearly empty pack before walking slowly into the snow-dusted forest. He made his way up the slope to the hill overlooking the creek where he knew his friends waited. Both of them whipped their slings over their heads and hurled rocks into the fast-moving water below to pass the time. They stopped when they heard him trudging through the snow.

"What did he say?" Vagrul asked.

Petrovisk slumped to the ground, folding his slender legs beneath his haunches. "I will not be at the fire tonight. I will leave the land of the greyshalks."

Andrusk growled in frustration. "The full moon has not come! Go out again."

Petrovisk twitched his ears downward, telling his friend "no."

"We will help you," Andrusk said. "Three

greyshalks will find something even in winter. Three spears will not fail. The clan will never know we helped you."

For such a deception, the spirits would never return. They had truly abandoned him on the seven hunts he had attempted on his own. Every time he got close to making a kill, the animal or the entire herd spooked and ran before he could cast his spear. When he could even find something to hunt. The deer were not in the beds where they often slept during the day, and the elk did not follow their usual paths. It was not bad luck. The spirits were against him, though he did not know what he had done to anger them. Petrovisk's nose burned as a tear crept from his eye and wet the short fur on his cheek.

"Stop that," Andrusk said. "Greyshalks must not leak like man people. Greyshalks keep the pain inside." He touched his thick fingers to the pelt of thick fur covering his chest. "You watch the man people too much and speak their words to the wind instead of hunting. There is no spirit magic in man words. They make you weak."

Petrovisk wiped the tear from his face. He was weak. One of the smallest in the clan, barely over six feet tall after fifteen summers, and his father was one of the largest, though Petrovisk's mother said Grawlin had gotten his growth spurt later than many others. Regardless, Andrusk was right. He should have hunted big game with the pack of older hunters so he could claim more meat from the kills. Instead he spent too many days in the summer filling his belly with plants and roots, singing the memory songs to himself while watching the man people across the river. His friends deserved to know what his father had said. He would tell them, because he would not see them again. "Andrusk, Vagrul, there is no way for me to stay. The hunter spirits are gone from me."

Vagrul growled at him, then whipped a stone from his sling. It hummed as it zipped through the air and splashed into the river. "Orc shit! You were your father's heir! You are not the worst hunter in the clan. The spirits have always been strong with you."

But not when it mattered most, Petrovisk thought.

"What of Alenka?" Andrusk asked. "Her insides will die if you leave."

"Better for her insides to die now," Petrovisk said. "Tell her I left on my own, as a greyshalk, and not some weak pursamank."

His friends winced.

Vagrul sat in the snow and wrapped his sling slowly around his forearm.

Andrusk bit his lower lip and sat down as well. "Where will you go? The tribe has all the land from here to the mountains of the Pyberian dwarves. They will not let you live there. Everything south is Beyklan. When they find you lurking around their pastures, they will send soldiers to kill you, and they will put your head on a spear and carry it to one of their places of many stone tents."

Petrovisk twitched his ears upward, telling them "yes," they were right. He thought about going toward the sea, which was not far from the camp. He could follow a stream and be there in three sunrises, maybe less. "I will go to the coast and make a canoe. I will paddle north to the ice lands across the angry sea."

Andrusk laughed. "You are a clever greyshalk, but you don't know how to make a canoe that will cross so much water. You'll just sink and drown. The sea is angry in winter, not some lake any greyshalk can cross."

Petrovisk's breath and some mucous came coarsely out of his wide, black nostrils. "I don't know where to go. Maybe if I sleep at the fork of a creek, in the sacred place of splitting paths, Great Shakkarn will send me a dream to show me which path to follow."

They sat in silence for a while until Andrusk grabbed Petrovisk by his shoulders. "At the fire tonight, we will sing the sacred words for you, my friend. But once you leave, we can never speak to you again or say your name in the memory songs."

Petrovisk sat in the snow as Vagrul and Andrusk got to their feet and made their way down the hill. Their friendship and the life they shared together was over.

Before all the light had gone from the sky, Petrovisk found a fork in the creek and stopped for the night. He leaned against a gnarled pine tree and watched the water flow away from him in two different directions. The tree stopped some of the wind, but he was cold in the darkness, and his blanket helped only a little. He did not deserve a fire, and the flames might frighten away the water spirits whose help he sought. If they were pleased, they would bring the nomad and great hunter, Shakkarn, to favor him, but if the spirits had all abandoned him as his father said, what chance was there of a god coming to his aid? He chanted the song of the greyshalk hunter who was lost and sought to find the way until he fell asleep, curled up on the frozen ground.

In the morning when he awoke, he knew the spirits of his people had truly deserted him, because he could not remember any of his dreams.

Petrovisk chose the familiar trails of the southeast and hiked until he came to the partially frozen river bordering the land claimed by the warlike and clever men of Beykla. They used spears and arrows tipped with iron and killed greyshalks who dared enter their homeland. He would avoid entering their territory for now and look for game to feed himself, hoping the animals had come down from the slopes of Mount Skarpas, the tall peak overshadowing the entire area.

He walked as quietly as he could and approached from downwind the likely hiding places deer would sleep during the day, but the animals avoided him. The hunting spirits truly had forsaken him, as they had all winter. The only prey he found in two days was a blackbird with an injured wing perched in a dead pine tree. It had taken two stones from his sling to finally knock the madly squawking bird from its perch. He roasted it over a small fire and had eaten all but the feathers and feet when he heard something moving in the snow beyond a nearby tree. He readied his spear as a tiny man pup appeared.

The creature had a pale bald face and long hair of an orange-red color Petrovisk had never seen before. He had watched many of the man folk over the seasons, mostly in spring and summer when they worked their large garden fields near the river. What was this youngling doing wandering around by itself in greyshalk territory?

"Heya," the pup said, lifting a tiny pale hand in greeting, its moss-colored eyes wide and very curious.

Petrovisk had a rudimentary grasp of the Beyklan language, though speaking their words was a challenge.

"Hehhhhah," he said.

The pup showed his teeth, and Petrovisk wondered if the little thing was trying to threaten him. Was this a trap, and the Beyklans had sent a pup to distract him as they prepared to attack? His clan had done such things in the past, sending a young greyshalk to lure enemies in close, because if they saw how tall the greyshalk warriors were they would be extremely wary.

He glanced at the woods and sniffed the air, angry that the smoke from his fire and the charred blackbird feathers made it difficult to focus on the scents around him. He smelled only this one small pup and he could not tell if it were male or female. Man folk looked the same, but he could usually tell them apart by their odor.

At least this one was no threat. He rested the butt of his spear on the ground.

The pup showed his teeth even wider and let out what he thought was the greyshalk equivalent of a laugh. It dawned on Petrovisk that it was not showing its teeth out of anger, but was greeting him as he had seen the man folk do before. He motioned for it to come closer, and as it did, he realized he could fit its tiny skull in his hand. He could crush it like a melon, and cook what little meat was on its bones.

The Beyklan pup suddenly rushed Petrovisk and wrapped its little arms around his leg. It wasn't trying to hurt him—it clung to him like a youngling clutching its mother's fur.

Petrovisk scooped up the pup in his arms and tried not to think about eating it. The little thing was quite ugly, the pale skin on its face and the back of its hands speckled with spots. It was so strange to look at its baldness up close—from what he knew of man folk they only had hair on their heads and genitals. He had seen them washing in the river numerous times and knew how to tell the difference then. He could strip the pup to determine its gender, but it wore odd animal skins and had fur-lined boots to keep warm. He could already feel it shivering, and its nose and hands were very cold as it snuggled against him. Stripping it would make it even colder and it might think he was going to skin and eat it.

Petrovisk cradled the pup as best he could and sat down. He offered it the crispy feet of the blackbird, the only parts he had saved. The hungry little thing chewed them up quickly and still looked famished. Petrovisk was hungry too.

"Thank you," the pup said in a high-pitched voice he found very endearing.

"Well-koom," Petrovisk said, then questioned if he had remembered the proper Beyklan response. He thought he knew what the words meant, but he could not be sure. His stomach still felt empty and the thought crossed his mind he would have a full belly if he only . . . no, he could not do that. Not now.

He let the pup sit on his leg, and realized that if any of his clan saw him treating it like a pet and not killing it on the spot, he would be slaughtered. If the pup were a full grown man who had entered greyshalks territory, he should have killed it and brought back the meat and the skull for a trophy to be placed at the base of the totem tree. His tribe would likely approve, but man folk were not sacred to the greyshalks, and would not bring strength to the clan or allow him to complete his rite of passage. He could not pass his kudekah by killing only a man, or even three, let alone this pitifully tiny creature.

They sat by the fire and Petrovisk wondered where the pup had come from. Was it lost? He hadn't been to this ground since last summer and man folk could have built a log tent inside greyshalk territory. The clan's hunters did not come here much, as larger game could be found elsewhere, and this was close to the territory of the greyshalks' smaller cousins, the vicious hyena-headed kriel. Would the man folk be foolish enough to live in such a place? They could have come across the river, but if the greyshalks or the kriel discovered they were nearby, they would kill them for sure.

The little pup giggled again and pulled on Petrovisk's chin hair. He felt sorry for it, and maybe he could help it find its kin. He touched its skull and pet its long reddish hair. The pup seemed to want to play with him, and man pups were such interesting creatures. He thought about keeping it and taking it with him when he searched for a new place to live and hunt.

The pup patted its little chest and looked up at him. "Angelique," it said, and repeated it a few times, as it wanted him to say something in return. He had never heard the word before, but assumed it was the little pup's name. It was a very beautiful word and reminded him of Alenka. Maybe it was a female pup?

"Petrovisk," he said, and pointed to his chest.

"Peter-fesk," the pup said and showed its teeth again.

He twitched his ears, "no," and said his name again, but he didn't understand if the pup recognized the gesture or knew he had given it his name.

Angelique hugged him, and held on tight as Petrovisk stood. He would find the pup's kin and leave him, or her, with them. He tracked the pup's footprints in the snow until the trees thinned out and he lost the trail on a frozen lake. He circled the lake, staying in greyshalk territory and wondered if he might find a place where a Beyklan would build a log tent on the bank. He could not find any more of the pup's prints and soon the day turned to a cold night. Petrovisk curled up under a tree and built a small fire, allowing the pup to snuggle against him. He would keep it warm, and in the morning would search for the Beyklans who must have lost it.

Or was it like him and had been sent away by its kin because it was a failure? No it was too young to be cast out. Petrovisk fell asleep remembering when he was so small he rode on his mother's back when they traveled from one camp to another. He would never see her again, and he would never see Alenka.

Petrovisk awoke to a man voice calling out a familiar word over and over.

"Annn-ge-leeek!" The word echoed through the trees.

The Beyklan pup was still asleep as Petrovisk got to his feet. He carried the tiny, sleeping creature toward the voice, which was beyond the trees a short distance from where they had slept, but still in greyshalk territory. He smelled a man, a horse, and something else—deer meat?—on the wind. He spotted a man riding a large black horse with white markings on its neck. The man was desperate or bold to risk his life coming across the river, and Petrovisk knew the reason was sleeping and tucked into the crook of his arm.

The rider did not see him, and Petrovisk hid in the trees, as he was expert at not being seen, and watched the Beyklan for a moment. The man wore a long cloak, which covered his shoulders and the flanks of the horse.

Petrovisk walked into the open and held the sleeping pup in front of him, lifting it and calling out, "Hehhhhah, Beyklan!"

The pup woke up squirming and almost fell from

his grasp. Petrovisk didn't want it to strike the hard ground and hurt itself, as man pups seemed so fragile. He held on tight and strode forward, his large feet tramping down the half-frozen yellow grass.

The man turned quickly, and his horse spooked upon seeing the greyshalk approaching. The Beyklan managed to steady his mount, and reached for a small bow, a weapon the size a greyshalk pup younger than him would play with. The man aimed a deadly-looking arrow with metal tip at Petrovisk.

The greyshalk continued forward, very slowly, and tried to remember the right words. He finally said, "Beyklan. Take . . . " He raised the pup, as he did not know what to call it in the Beyklan language.

The man's eyes narrowed as he aimed carefully.

Petrovisk wished he had not left his spear back at his camp. This was going to be a fight to the death, as it often was when mankind and greyshalks met each other.

Petrovisk tuned sideways, preparing to dodge the arrow, and held Angelique on his hip, shielding it with his body.

The pup called out in fear, probably afraid of being shot. Petrovisk thought of the Beyklan words to stop this. "No fight," Petrovisk said. "Take."

The still squirming pup said something and tried to slip out of Petrovisk's grasp. He let it go and watched in amazement as the pup ran from him to the Beyklan. The rider scooped the youngling up and held it close.

Petrovisk thought about fleeing as the man put away his bow, but curiosity got the better of him.

Watching man people this close was quite rare.

The pup and the man exchanged words so rapidly Petrovisk understood nothing. When the words were over, the pup waved, as if saying farewell.

The man said, "Thank you for taking care of my daughter."

Petrovisk did not understand all the words, but he knew what some of them meant. 'Daughter' was a word he had heard before. It meant young female man folk. Angelique had to be a girl. Petrovisk nodded and said, "Well-koom."

The man seemed surprised, but the pup giggled, and said something urgent. He nodded at her and reached into a sack hanging from his leather seat atop the horse. Petrovisk noticed the rider had thick orange-red hair that circled his mouth and grew toward his pink ears. The color of his hair was similar to Angelique's.

The Beyklan pulled a large bundle from a sack, and gestured toward Petrovisk, then tossed it on the ground. The rider touched his heels to the horse and it stepped away from the bundle. Petrovisk approached what the man had dropped, which smelled like deer meat and something else. Petrovisk unwrapped it, sniffing at the man-made cloth covering it and was surprised to find several large hunks of dried venison inside. He licked a piece and loved the sweet and sharp flavor. He took a bite. It was better than any dried meat he had ever eaten. Something more than salt had been applied to it, maybe wild onion and something else he could not identify.

"Thonk-yooo," Petrovisk said, hoping the meat

would last him several days.

"You're welcome," the man said.

"Peter-fesk," the pup said, showing his teeth.

"Ann-ge-leek," Petrovisk said, and showed his teeth, but he did not mean it as a threat. He liked the ugly girl pup. She would have made a good pet, but it was better for her to be with her kin.

She waved as the rider turned his horse and went south through the meadow. He hoped the man would take Angelique back to Beyklan territory. If they stayed in the land of the greyshalks, or strayed to the kriel hunting grounds, it would not end well.

The young greyshalk hiked through the foothills of Mount Skarpas, his backpack filled with the venison he had received for saving the girl pup. The food would last only a few days, but he would find a way around the mountain and go down to the coastline on the other side. Whenever his clan had made camp on the coast he had been one of the best fishers, or at least better than Vagrul and Andrusk. He could smell clams under the beach sand better than them as well. He was confident he would catch or find enough food and he loved the taste of the seaweed that washed onto the shore every day. He would build a warm shelter with a view of the sea, and he might even build a canoe. When he had enough dry fish, he would go south until he left the greyshalks' territory forever. He would become an explorer, and none would ever see him—unless he wanted them to.

Petrovisk would be a ghost, a myth, and the greyshalks would hear stories of him, and wonder if it was Petrovisk who had done such wondrous things. He daydreamed about the places he would go and all that he would do as he hiked beside a gurgling stream, which he hoped would lead him to the sea.

A shadow passing overhead drew his attention, and when he looked up he expected to see a lone cloud in the clear winter sky. His eyes widened as the gigantic rikr-eagle flew overhead. Clutched in its talons was a black horse with a white patch on its neck.

The same horse Angelique had been taken away on! The rikr-eagle had killed the animal, but what about the little girl pup? Before he realized what he was doing, Petrovisk sprinted after the giant raptor. He had no idea what he was going to do or how he would catch up to it.

The rikr-eagle flew toward a stony ridge on a spur of Mount Skarpas. He watched it circle around to the other side of the mountain and disappear. It must have landed on a ledge and gone to a nest, which had to be in the rocky tower in the shadow of the snowcapped peak.

Gasping for air, Petrovisk reached the top of a steep slope and fell to his knees. He rubbed snow on his face and asked himself what he was doing. The girl pup was not on the mountain. She was with her people, who had just lost a horse. He would not climb Mount Skarpas for a girl pup. Why was he even considering such a foolish thing?

Had he just found a way to prove himself and

rejoin the clan?

The final full moon of winter was three weeks away. He had time to climb the mountain and find a way to kill the rikr-eagle. If he did such an incredible feat, his clan would honor him, and remember his kudekah in the memory songs forever. Only one greyshalk had killed a rikr-eagle in the history of his people. He knew the song of the great hunter, Ludrok the Swift, founder of the Feather Clan, who lived in the distant north. Their totem tree still had the feather of the rikr-eagle Ludrok himself had tied to it generations ago, but no other clans would dare enter their territory even now, so potent was their spirit magic.

Petrovisk would see his family again, his father would be proud, and Alenka would be his mate. Their clan would be known, and they would have many feathers of the rikr-eagle, whose spirit would stay with Petrovisk and give him great power. He would be the most skilled hunter, able to see prey from far distances, and so fast of foot nothing could escape him. The power of the giant bird would be his. If only he could climb the icy mountain and find the nest. He would wait until it slept, then plunge his spear through its eye and claim his trophies.

Filled with purpose, Petrovisk trekked to the base of the mountain. He killed a pair of white hares with his sling and saved their skins, fashioning them into sacks to cover his hands in the night. He spent two days searching for a way up the icy ledge where the rikr-eagle nested, and narrowly avoided being caught in an avalanche on the slope beneath it.

On his third day sleeping on the mountain he could not keep his fire lit because he ran out of wood in the middle of the night. Ice clung to his fur by morning, and he wondered if it was the cold, or growing pains that made his bones ache so much. He ate the last of the venison and it warmed him, or perhaps it was the rising sun when he crawled from the small cave where he had sheltered. He carefully watched the ledge far above, wondering if the great bird were still in the nest. His patience had nearly run out when the raptor leaped from its roost shortly before midday. Petrovisk waited until it circled to the other side of Mount Skarpas before attempting the climb. The raptor had returned late in the afternoon each of the past three days, and he hoped he would have enough time to get into position for a kill.

He began to climb the nearly sheer slope, his short spear tied to his back. The route he had seen to the top proved passable as he started his ascent. He followed a crack in the rock using his long reach and his greyshalk strength to find excellent handholds, and when necessary, he dangled by one arm as he reached forward. He made it halfway up the cliff before he could find no way ahead. Frustrated, he climbed back down and found a different way only to be stopped again on an exposed rock face by an overhang blocking the route above him.

Fear began to gnaw at him, and he paused, hoping to see a way up as he searched for handholds. Long moments passed and he knew he should not linger in such an exposed place. The wind gusted and he flattened himself against the mountain, waiting for the weather to calm, and letting the sun warm his frozen fingers. When the breeze finally quieted he realized the rest had done him more good than he realized. His courage had returned, and he pressed on, refusing to let the mountain defeat him. Petrovisk found a handhold on the underside of the ceiling above him and swung out over the drop-off, dangling above the icy, boulder-strewn slope far below.

Petrovisk had to let one of his hands go to reach around the lip of the overhang. He could not find a place to grab on. The grip he had with his other hand was slipping. If he fell, his body would be broken and lost, frozen in the snow atop the mountain. There would be no rejoining his clan or giving his spirit to them. He would fail another kudekah, his last. He reached even further, stretching to the limit. His fingers curled around a protruding bit of rock. He pulled himself up and over and did not stop climbing until he found secure footholds. He held in a howl of joy as he realized the rikr-eagle's gigantic nest of tree trunks and boulders was right above him.

He glanced over his shoulder at the peak of Mount Skarpas, and scanned the sky for the rikr-eagle. He had seen it fly toward the coast and guessed it would not return for hours, giving him plenty of time to prepare his trap. He climbed the rest of the way and found bits of wood, and a piece of elk carcass wedged into crevice. He ate the meat off the bone and sucked out the marrow. The smell of rotting meat above him made him hunger for more, but the overpowering stench of the rikr-eagle, which reminded him of goose droppings, and made his nose itch.

He climbed over the side of the nest, mostly made up of the trunks of dead pine trees, masts from what had to be sailing ships, and several large rocks carried from the land below. He peered inside the bowl where the rikr-eagle slept and saw the remains of deer, elk, moose, bear, cattle, horses, sheep, and what Petrovisk imagined were giant fish or sharks. He even spotted the tiny skull of a man. The rikr-eagle had also collected several pieces of metal. He climbed down into the nest and inspected the bits of Beyklan armor ripped from the bodies of the rikr-eagle's prey. He wondered how he could shape the metal into cutting tools.

Then he saw it. The large axe was half-buried by snow in the bottom of the nest. Petrovisk lifted the weapon and felt the weight. He could heft it easily, but the wickedly sharp and head of tapered metal would bite deep through a tree or an enemy. The long oak handle was slender in his hand, but it would do well enough. He wondered what race had crafted it. No rust blemished the blade, as he had seen the red dust on all of the iron weapons a few hunters in his clan carried. This must be of a different metal, the legendary steel that the dwarves of the Pyberian Mountains crafted in their caverns deep in the ground. Or was it a weapon of the minotaur folk, who were said to be as large as the greyshalks.

Petrovisk pondered the mysteries of his new axe as he searched the large nest. He found several black feathers with white tips that were taller than he was. He would tie at least three of them to the clan's totem tree.

Or should he wait for the rikr-eagle and tear feathers from its corpse after he killed it?

A high-pitched shriek came from the back of the nest, and Petrovisk jumped back, raising his axe. He heard it again and realized there was an opening in the mountain behind the nest, like a natural tent of two gigantic slabs of stone. The rikr-eagle could not fit in such a small space, but . . .

The rikr-eagle chick came out of the opening, its eyes locked on him as if he were food. The monster, taller than he was, spread its wings and let out a piercing screech that hurt his ears. The hungry eaglet lunged at him, snapping with a hooked beak that gouged into a tree trunk.

Petrovisk swung his axe at the monster and growled, but it was not intimidated and pressed its attack, dodging his blows quite easily. He jumped out of the way of another attack as a second rikr-eagle chick came out of the hiding place at the rear of the nest.

The pair surrounded him as he swung the axe in circles, fending off their lightning-fast beaks. They flapped their wings, taking flight and slashing at him with their talons. The eaglets pressed him toward the cave where they had come from, and Petrovisk smelled rotting meat and freshly killed horse inside —and something else.

A third rikr-eaglet struck at Petrovisk from the shadows, but he expected the attack and used his axe to fend it off. When the bird came out, Petrovisk split its skull with an overhand chop.

The wounded bird stumbled forward and he

severed its head. The sharpness of the axe left him staring at the blade.

The other eaglets stared on their dead nest-mate, and one of them seized the head and pulled it away from Petrovisk. The young rikr-eagle dropped its prize and pecked at the bloody neck meat. Soon they were both tearing off strips of flesh and gulping them down.

Petrovisk left them to eat the body of the dead bird. He thought of staying and trying to kill the pair of rikr-eaglets, but when he looked at them, they stopped and met his gaze with their orange-yellow eyes, daring him to challenge them. He had killed the smallest of them, and the two remaining birds were larger, faster, and hungrier than he was.

Faced with the cruel monsters, the young greyshalk did what he had to do and fled. It was a dream to even think he could kill a full-grown rikr-eagle, but before he escaped the nest, Petrovisk grabbed the largest feather he could find.

The climb down the cliff was much harder than coming up. The axe and the feather, and his spear on his back threw off his balance. His strength was waning, and he knew that if he did not get down soon, the rikr-eagle would return and pluck him off the cliff. He almost fell three times before he decided to drop everything he carried. Without the weapons and the feather, he climbed better, but his fingers were like blocks of ice, and his muscles trembled.

All his courage left him with his strength, but he kept going, heart pounding like a drum until he reached the base of the cliff. When he reached the bottom he could hardly believe he had survived. The spirits must have been with him, or perhaps Shakkarn himself.

He recovered the feather, the axe and his spear, and none of them had been damaged, another blessing. He hustled to the small cave where he had spent the previous night, while looking over his shoulder for the rikr-eagle, who he thought would appear in the sky at any moment.

The raptor bird appeared when Petrovisk had only a dozen steps more to reach his shelter, and he forgot how to breathe. He dropped to his knees and pretended to be a rock, until the bird disappeared inside the large nest. Petrovisk sprinted the last few steps and scuttled inside the cave.

The screeching of the rikr-eagle echoed off the mountain for an impossibly long time. He hoped it wouldn't know he had even gone to the nest, but he heard another call, and the flapping of wings. It sounded like it was getting closer and he imagined it was following his footprints over the snowy ridge and right to the cave.

He pressed himself as far inside the shallow cave as he could while the pounding wing beats came closer and closer. The ground shook as the gigantic raptor landed right above him. The earth shook and bits of ice fell on him. Petrovisk held his breath hoping it would go away, but he was a rabbit gone to ground, and the predator knew right where he was.

The rikr-eagle reached inside his shallow cave with the talons on one of its bulbous feet. Petrovisk tried to burrow into the rock and for the first time in his life, wished he was much smaller.

A long black talon tore a gash in his leg, and he barely avoided being dragged from his hole. The rikr-eagle reached in again and again, and though Petrovisk could not swing the axe properly in the confined space, he waited for the next attack and chopped hard enough to sever the tip of one of the monster's clawed toes.

Blood spurted on him as the rikr-eagle pulled out its foot and flew away. Petrovisk kept the sharp talon and ate the small piece of flesh. The bony claw was longer than his forearm and the tip so sharp he thought it might scratch stone. His clan would be amazed at the feather, but when he showed them the rikr-eagle claw, they would be awed. If he carried such a potent talisman, the spirits would have to return to him, if they hadn't already.

The wind howled all through the night as Petrovisk lay awake in the small cave on Mount Skarpas, his leg bleeding and throbbing with pain. He used the rikr-eagle feather to block the entrance, and was surprised at how well the thick feather kept out the freezing air. Still, he slept little as he remembered his harrowing descent from the nest and all that had happened.

Before sunrise, Petrovisk crept from the cave. He limped down the mountain and arrived in the foothills before the rikr-eagle left its nest. He watched it circle the ridge where he had slept, and when it couldn't find him, the bird flew over the mountain and toward the sea, likely to hunt for less dangerous prey.

He dragged the feather behind him, tying the white bony tip to his waist and retracing his steps out of the foothills. He stopped at a stream to drink and managed to catch three trout by stabbing them with his spear. He ate them raw, bones and all, and kept going after putting moss on his leg wound and wrapping it with a fresh piece of deer hide he took from his backpack. His injury was not severe, and he would heal in a few days, though the scar would remain to remind him of how close he had come to death.

Petrovisk planned to go straight to his clan's camp and present his trophies to the elders at the totem tree and ask to be recognized as a kip. None could say he had failed another kudekah, and they would recognize him as a warrior and hunter at last. He would see Alenka and she would throw her arms around him and welcome him back. Her family would offer her as his mate, and they would have many pups together.

The sun shone on Petrovisk as he hiked for home. He almost enjoyed the ache in his leg. He basked in the bright sunlight as the sky cleared and the snow began to melt. Winter was ending, but he had many sunrises left before the last full moon of the season.

On the second day of his journey home he came across tracks in the snow leading away from his clan's camp. Three greyshalks at least, and one of them was female by the smell and the size of her prints. He couldn't be sure, but it reminded him of Alenka's scent. Had she gone on a hunt with her father and uncle? He followed the tracks and realized he was near the field where he had returned Angelique to the rider.

Had they been following his own trail? The possibility made the fur on his back stand on end.

Why would they have come for him? Had Alenka convinced her father to help her find him so they could return home together? Or had they come to relieve him of his pelt and make sure he would never trouble them again?

Cautiously, Petrovisk entered the field and spotted many tracks trampling over those of the three greyshalks. He smelled the ground and knew at once by the odor and the size, that they were kriel. The smaller hyena headed cousins of the greyshalks were tracking his kin. He had to warn them before the larger group of kriel attacked, if they hadn't already. He guessed there were at least six of them, and ran after the tracks now, dragging the feather behind him.

The faint smell of woodsmoke on the breeze made him run faster. He took long strides and ignored the pain in his thigh, though fresh blood dripped down his leg. He found the frozen lake and spotted where a horse had crossed. The greyshalk and kriel tracks followed the horse's faint hoof marks, which led toward a column of rising smoke on the far side, in Beyklan territory.

He thought about leaving the feather in greyshalk territory, but changed his mind. His enemies might find it and claim the totem for themselves. He would keep the feather with him and defend it with his life.

Petrovisk entered Beyklan territory through a stand of pine trees and found a field that had been cleared of brush. At the far end of the open area he spotted two Beyklan huts made of logs. The roof of the smaller hut was on fire, and Petrovisk hoped this was not the place where Angelique and the rider lived.

Had the kriel attacked? He approached cautiously and spotted a small wolf-like creature laying dead in the yard. Bright red blood stained the snow and he realized it could not have been dead for very long. It was half the size of a wolf, more like a fox, but with a strange coat of shaggy white fur. It looked like it would be good to eat, and Petrovisk thought about snatching up the unattended kill, but it was too dangerous to rush ahead.

The smoke masked the scents of whatever else was there, and the kriel tracks went toward the huts. Petrovisk circled in the trees and spotted another dead body. It was furry, reddish brown with spots, and was smaller than a greyshalk. He had seen them once before, but from a long way off. The kriel were much smaller and weaker than the greyshalks, but they ran in packs and were deadly enemies. The kriel lay on its back outside the larger hut. An arrow protruded from its eye.

Petrovisk ducked behind a tree and watched for more kriel and the archer. He untied the giant feather from his waist and put it down. It would get in the way if he fought, though if his enemies saw it, they might run in fear once they realized what powerful spirits were with him. He readied his spear and axe and considered his sling wrapped around his wrist. There were a few good stones within reach.

A creature stepped out of the larger wooden hut and looked around, sniffing the air. It was partially hunched over and had light reddish brown fur with dark brown spots on its shoulders. The kriel held a war club in one hand and carried a stone axe in the other. Perhaps he should sneak away before it saw him and try to find the trail of the three greyshalks?

A larger figure came out of the hut and Petrovisk gasped. It was his father dragging the bloody body of a wo-man.

The kriel pointed and laughed at the corpse.

Grawlin licked his lips. "We roast this one. Mark our hunt together with cooked meat."

"Kriel and greyshalks will hunt many Beyklans in season ahead," the kriel said in a high-pitched voice. "Tonight we bury the man-skulls, and say sacred words together, join our clans with blood of enemies."

Petrovisk was stunned. Hunting with the kriel was forbidden by the memory songs. Greyshalk and kriel must never join together or the ancestor spirits would be angry, as would Shakkarn the Hunter. His father was a shaman, he knew better than anyone. This would destroy the clan.

Should Petrovisk slink away from this and tell the clan chiefs? He crouched lower, preparing to sneak away when a shrill girl pup cry made his ears swivel toward the large hut.

"Run Angelique!" a man shouted.

Petrovisk knew it was the rider, Angelique's father.

The shrill cry came again and Petrovisk knew he had to do something. Had she been hiding and now the kriel found her? He would distract them and hope she escaped. The ugly little pup did not deserve to die so young. He grabbed the giant rikr-eagle feather and stepped into the open. Petrovisk planted the bony end of the feather in the ground, and made the howling battle cry of the greyshalks as loud as he could.

When the kriel and greyshalks turned from the commotion inside the big hut to look at him, he held his axe and spear over his head and howled at them again, baring his teeth.

His father howled back and showed his teeth.

"Who is this kip greyshalk yowling at us?" the surprised kriel asked, as three more of his kind joined him.

"He is nothing," Grawlin said. "He is banished from the clan. A worthless mouth to feed."

Petrovisk planted his spear in the ground opposite the feather, hoping to give Angelique a chance at survival. "No, I am Petrovisk, kip of Grawlin," he pointed at his father, "the shaman of our clan."

"Kip of Grawlin?" the kriel asked, quite surprised.

Grawlin huffed out his cheeks and wrinkled his nose. "I do not claim him as kip of my clan."

"Father, I have returned after my kudekah," Petrovisk said. "I climbed Mount Skarpas and stole a rikr-eagle feather. I killed one of the rikr-eaglets in its nest and I chopped this talon from the rikr-eagle itself!" He held up the long claw.

The kriel cackled and yipped. "He is great warrior! Kip of Grawlin!"

"No, he shames the greyshalks," his father said.

The kriel looked confused.

Petrovisk pointed at the feather. "I have completed my kudekah. I will return to the camp and claim Alenka as my mate."

Grawlin laughed and called to another greyshalk inside the wooden hut. A greyshalk came out and Petrovisk immediately recognized Alenka's father, Magroul Bone Taker.

The old greyshalk licked blood from his fingers and eyed Petrovisk with hatred, and glanced at the rikr-eagle feather, a hint of surprise in his yellow eyes.

Grawlin whispered to Magroul and the aged greyshalk laughed.

"You will never have Alenka," Magroul said, pointing a bloody finger at Petrovisk.

"No. I will take her. I have the rikr feather and Alenka will be my mate."

The pack of four kriel laughed and as a group dragged Alenka from the hut, as it took all of them to overpower her. She had been inside the whole time. Her eyes found Petrovisk and she tried to crawl to him, but her father stepped on her spine and pressed her into the ground. The corded muscle of his leg bulged and Alenka cried out in pain.

"Because of you, Alenka would not take any of the clan as her mate," Magroul said. "I gave her to Andrusk, but she refused him and bit half his ear off. Greyshalk female who does this is worthless. I have given her to the kriel, and she will give them many strong pups. The biggest they have ever had."

The pack of kriel cackled and barked as they gathered around her, marking her fur with their anal glands.

"She will not go to them!" Petrovisk shouted, and

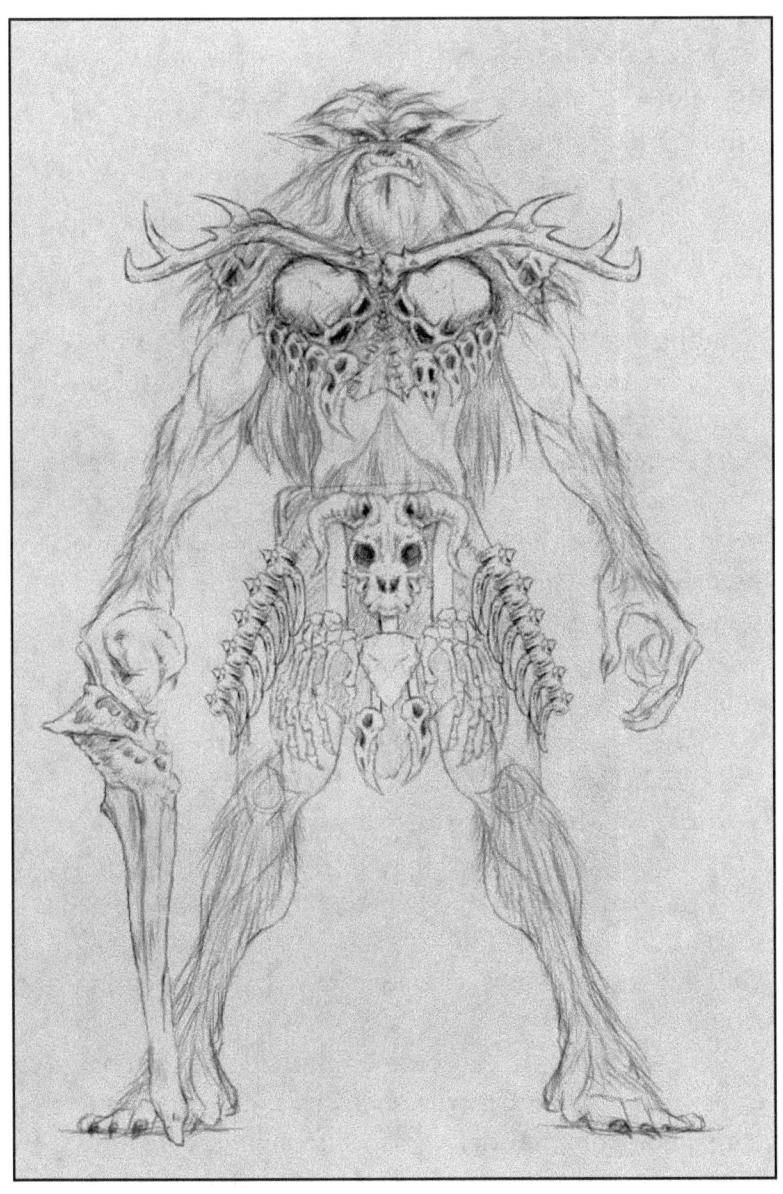

"Magroul Bone Taker" by Kendall R. Hart

raised his axe.

The four kriel howled. They raised their stone axes and clubs. Their leader shouted, "Greyshalk female is ours to mate with. She is price of peace between us."

"No!" Petrovisk shouted.

"It's done," Grawlin said. "We have shed blood on a hunt with our kriel cousins. The peace is settled."

"These Beyklans were killed so our clan could join with the kriel?" Petrovisk asked, his anger building.

"Your tracks led us here," Grawlin said, gesturing to the huts.

Petrovisk had brought this destruction to the Beyklans. He was enraged. "These are not our lands or the lands of the kriels. You should not have come here. The chiefs will be angry when they hear what you have done."

"The chiefs sent us here, you foolish pup!" Grawlin shouted. "The chiefs listen to my council, not yours!"

"The Beyklans did not threaten the greyshalks!" Petrovisk shouted. Killing them was wrong. Turning against the old ways would lead the greyshalks into danger.

The shaman growled at his son and kicked the woman's body in front of him. "We'll eat this one tonight," Grawlin said, and motioned for a kriel to get something from inside the hut.

The krill carried out something small with a shock of orange-red hair. Grawlin snatched the body of little Angelique from the kriel's grasp and carried her toward Petrovisk. In his other hand he held his shaman's war staff, carved with many greyshalk faces, like the totem tree. When the shaman stood in front of Petrovisk, he dropped the girl pup in a mud puddle. She rolled onto her back. Her moss colored eyes were dull and lifeless. "I will take this pup to the chiefs and show them I did what they asked."

The kriel all barked and prodded Alenka with their clubs.

Rage like nothing Petrovisk had ever felt coursed though him. Time seemed to slow. He raised his axe and chopped at his father with all his might. Grawlin tried to turn the blow aside with his shaman's war staff, but the axe cut through the wood and split his father's face in two halves. Petrovisk kept chopping until the skull was a bloody mess.

Magroul snarled and charged to avenge the fallen shaman.

No greyshalk could stand against Magroul Bone Taker. Not even if Petrovisk carried an axe of true steel.

Magroul hurled his spear at Petrovisk after his running start, but the young greyshalk dodged, and the shaft flew past his shoulder.

A few more steps and the mighty greyshalk warrior would kill him.

Petrovisk dropped his axe. He snatched his flint spear out of the ground, and prepared to make to make the most important throw of his life.

Magroul raised his iron-studded war club for a killing blow as Petrovisk dug his toes into the cold ground and threw his flint spear with all his might.

Alenka's father was only a two strides away and could not avoid the sharp tip, which pierced his gut. He stopped running and stared at the shaft. He dropped his war club and let out an angry growl as he locked his hands around the shaft.

Petrovisk grabbed the butt of the spear and their eyes locked together. Magroul was more than a head taller and much stronger. He was old, but he was one of the toughest in the clan.

"I will kill you!" Magroul said, and tried to pull the spear out of his stomach.

Petrovisk howled and pushed as hard as he could, his feet finding solid ground while Magroul's found an icy patch and slipped backwards. The spear penetrated deeper, and Magroul reached for Petrovisk's throat with one giant hand.

The young greyshalk felt the leathery fingers grasp his throat, squeezing off his breath. Petrovisk pushed harder and wrenched the shaft form side to side as hard as he could.

The old greyshalk let go of Petrovisk and he fell on his back screaming in agony.

Petrovisk retreated and picked up his axe. He stood by the mortally wounded greyshalk, ready to cut off his head and end his suffering.

Magroul drew a rusty iron knife and cut Petrovisk's ankle.

Enraged more than hurt, the young greyshalk savagely crushed Magroul's hands and arms, using the top of the axe, flattening his enemy's fingers until they were broken and useless.

"The spirits will curse you!" Magroul shouted.

Petrovisk howled at him and used the flat of his axe

like a hammer to pound the spear through the fallen warrior until it erupted from Magroul's back. He struck it until it pinned Magroul to the ground.

When Petrovisk finally looked up, his face spattered with blood, two more of the kriel were dead. Alenka stood over their bodies holding a stone war club covered in gore.

He looked for the last of their enemies.

She pointed toward the woods behind the hut.

One of the kriel sprinted for the trees, but the other limped along holding its flank, as Alenka's bone knife was still sheathed up to the hilt.

Petrovisk and Alenka charged after them. She caught the wounded kriel at the edge of the trees and grabbed it by the scraggly hair on its head, pulling her knife from its back. The kriel made a yipping cry, which was abruptly silenced as she stabbed the side of its throat.

The kriel were fools to think they could have tamed her. She would have ruled their clan.

Petrovisk's wounded leg and ankle burned with pain as he sprinted after the kriel. He was taller and had longer strides, but the kriel was fast, and very afraid, judging by the scat it had left behind.

The kriel stopped at the edge of a clearing and stared up at the sky. A large shadow passed overhead, but Petrovisk did not look up. He slammed his body into the much smaller foe and crushed him into the ground. Petrovisk turned him over and pressed his fingers into the kriel's eyes, which popped like overly ripe gooseberries.

The blind and wounded kriel shrieked as Petrovisk

snarled and bit through both bloodways on its neck. Hot blood poured from the wound, and the kriel died grasping at its throat.

The shadow overhead circled and Petrovisk recognized the shape of the rikr-eagle. He sprinted into the thicker forest and ran toward the last place he had seen Alenka. He found her at the edge of the trees, near the body of the last kriel she had killed.

The rikr-eagle had landed in the field, and the massive wings touched the edge of the trees. The monstrosity stared at Petrovisk, then wrapped its talons around Grawlin's body. It flapped its wings to take off, and the sound was like thunder in Petrovisk's chest. Snow and pine needles nearly blinded him as the rikr-eagle screeched and flew away toward Mount Skarpas.

The feather Petrovisk had stolen was knocked over, but it remained, while his father's body was taken. Was this a sign? A message from the spirits that Grawlin had been wrong about everything they had done and Petrovisk was right? There was no way for him to know, but he would not forget this. He would make up his own memory song.

"Petrovisk."

Someone said his name. He turned and saw Alenka stood there, the grey and brown fur on her breasts covered with a dusting of snow. She would soon be his mate.

"You . . . you killed them," she said, glancing at the place where the pair of greyshalk bodies had been lying a moment before. Now only Magroul's motionless body remained.

He did kill them, didn't he? He had killed both of their fathers. Two of the best hunters in the village. They had underestimated him. Petrovisk felt numb, and he tried to say something, but only a shocked groan came out of his mouth.

Alenka reached out, took his hand, and helped him stand. Sorrow filled her beautiful yellow eyes. "We can never go back."

We? he thought. "I cannot. You can. None of the clan must know about this."

"But I know," she said.

Petrovisk felt his heart sink. "They should not have done this to you or to the Beyklans who lived here."

"They were punished by the spirits," she said. "The spirits were waiting for this moment, to stop the alliance between the kriel and the greyshalks. The spirits have spoken through you. This was your kudekah."

Petrovisk had felt like an avalanche of snow had fallen on him when he left the clan, and now it was lifted. The spirits had worked through him. They had returned to him and were stronger than ever. How else was he able to defeat his own father and Magroul the Bone Taker? Alenka must be right. "But I did not save the Beyklans. I wanted to save the little girl pup, Ange-leek."

"One Beyklan still lives," Alenka said. "Come."

Petrovisk and Alenka ducked as they entered the hut. The other hut burned hot and smoke drifted around them. Petrovisk found a man on the floor—the rider—the father of Angelique, bound to a post. Blood dripped from his nose and he screamed at Petrovisk when he saw him. The man must have been vowing revenge against the kriel and greyshalks who had killed his mate and pup in front of him.

Petrovisk knelt in front of him so the man could see his face more easily. He bared his teeth, trying to imitate the expression ugly little Angelique had used.

The man seemed more angry and yelled louder.

The greyshalk said, "Peter-fesk," as Angelique had said it.

The man's mouth hung open, his eyes wide.

"Ann-ge-leek. Friend," Petrovisk said.

"Peter-fesk," the man said, realizing who he was at last.

Petrovisk cut the cords that held the man. The Beyklan stood slowly and stepped from the hut to where the bodies of his family had been thrown. Petrovisk followed and watched him cradle the body of his mate and his pup. The man cried and wailed. Great tears of sorrow drained from his face.

Alenka placed her hand on Petrovisk's arm. "I now know why Beyklan's let their eyes leak."

Petrovisk felt the terrible sadness of the man. He felt a burn in his nose and his eyes leaked too. He placed his arm around Alenka. The warmth of her body felt good, but he could not stop the sadness. "My eyes leak too," he said.

"Let's leave him to his mate and pup," she said. "He probably wants to eat them so they will live through him."

The pair of greyshalks walked to the rikr-eagle feather, because Petrovisk still planned to claim it.

Alenka's father was still alive. His eyelids opened when they stood over him.

"Alenka. Free me," he glanced at the spear. "Do not betray your clan. Do not become an outcast coward like this worthless pursamank."

"No, you are a coward," Alenka said. "You hunt with kriel and gave me to them as a mate for a whole pack! Their wickedness has blackened your spirit. No one will eat your flesh. It will rot on the earth and your power will be lost. You cannot stop me now. I will be the mate of Petrovisk."

"I should have killed him on his last kudekah," Magroul said.

"You were not on Mount Skarpas," Petrovisk said.

Magroul huffed. "I was in the forest on all your other kudekahs. Your father had me frighten the animals, make you fail."

"Father, why?" Alenka asked.

The dying warrior pressed his lips together, refusing to speak.

Petrovisk knew the reason. "My father knew I would sing the old songs to the elders, try to convince them to stop the blood bond with the kriel. I would have spoken for the old ways, the greyshalk ways."

"I told your father I should have killed you while you are so small," Magroul said, "before you tried to take over the clan."

"They thought you would grow as large as your father," Alenka said. "They thought you would challenge them."

"The greyshalks must abandon the old ways,"

Magroul said, "or our enemies will take our lands."

"If we abandon the old ways," Petrovisk said, "the spirits will abandon us, and we will not be greyshalks."

Magroul huffed, but his strength was fading as the ground drank his blood.

The Beyklan walked past Petrovisk and Alenka. He carried his mate's body over his shoulder and his pup's in his arms. He laid them by a nearby tree, propping them up so their faces were directed at Magroul.

The man stood over the dying greyshalk and pulled a small knife from his belt. It was curved on one end. He kneeled down next to Magroul, paused, and said something Petrovisk did not understand.

"What did he say?" Alenka asked.

"Perhaps he is offering us a chance to eat your father's flesh?"

"Tell him we will not," she said.

"Greyshalks not eat," Petrovisk said in Beyklan.

The man nodded, and sliced Magroul with his knife, starting at the spear wound in his gut. Magroul screamed and wailed as he was skinned alive.

Petrovisk watched and when Magroul was finally dead, he reclaimed his spear.

"Thank you," the man said.

"Well-koom," Petrovisk said, before he picked the rikr-eagle feather off the ground and led Alenka toward the territory of the greyshalks. He was troubled and did not know what to do. "Alenka, where do we go now? Should we tell the clan chiefs about what happened?"

"No. They want to make peace with the kriel and bury the blood bones with them."

"Why?" Petrovisk asked.

"I heard your father speaking to mine. He said that the orc tribes on the other side of the great river are fighting under one chief," Alenka said. "The far walkers told him a cunning orc shaman, small in size, but of great power, now leads them. Others say it is a giant."

"What will we do now?" he asked. The future so unknown to him.

"We will not return to our clan of greyshalks," she said. "We are not in the clan after what has happened. The spirits are with you, us, not them."

They walked in the woods as the sun slipped behind the clouds. Alenka found a dry place to make a fire in the shelter of many tall pine trees. Petrovisk leaned the rikr-eagle feather against a tree, unsure what to do with it now. Earlier that day he thought he would rejoin his clan, and that his kudekah was completed on Mount Skarpas, but it had been completed tonight, on a bloody field where he had killed his own kind. His own father, and his mate's. Petrovisk and Alenka would never go back. They were greyshalks no longer.

The fire crackled, warming their feet as Alenka draped her arm across his chest and put her head on his shoulder.

"Alenka," he said.

"Yes."

"If we are not in the clan," he said, "we must not have greyshalk names."

"What name will you take when we form our own clan?" she asked.

"You will choose my name," he said, "but I will call you Ann-ge-leek."

"Mungo the Giant" by Zachary Hill

Mungo the Undying
by Patrick M. Tracy

I am Mungo, son of Mogo, son of Bruug. This is a
story of the time when I worked for a sorcerer. Many
know of the days when I saved the Blue Lip tribe of
orcs. Many also know about my part in the rise of
Tezok the Witchdoctor of the Poison Spear Tribe, but
this tale is rarely told. Most who remember these days
are long gone, their bodies burned or eaten or buried
under stones. I tell it now to you, for I am old and my
time runs short. What I remember of those dark
times will be yours to carry forward. Let my words
not be forgotten.

I was dead when this story began.

No-Tusks' trickery had doomed me, and my body
was to be eaten by the orcs of the Iron Spear tribe. It was
a bad day. I had trusted in the clever little orc and that
led to my demise. For a moment, I had been chief of the
Ironspears, but No-Tusks had poisoned the wine, and
I had drunk deeply. This, of course, was not enough to
slay me. Few poisons can slay a giant of my size and
power. We can be weakened, however.

No-Tusks caused a trap of logs to fall upon my head,
and as the sharp spears poked into me, I fell into a deep
unconsciousness. When I awoke, they were pulling the

stones and logs from my body, many grinning orcs all around with sharpened cleavers and knives.

Some tell that they butchered and ate me that day, but that is not true. I was able to rise and stagger to the edge of their encampment. They stayed away, No-Tusks again the slave of the Kar. They had suffered much bloodshed, and No-Tusks assured them that my wounds and the poison would do me in. They hung back, and the darkness gathered in my eyes once more. I slid to the ground, face first in the mud. Though I was stronger than they thought, strong enough to almost escape, I was not quite strong enough.

Being dead, I did not have any thoughts, and so I was not sad or angry at myself for my foolishness. That would come later. Being dead is not so bad. It is like a quiet day in the forest when nothing happens. I will enjoy being dead when I do it again, I think.

While the orcs sharpened their knives and began preparing fires to roast my meat, a human arrived at their village. A sorcerer. He offered gold. The Ironspear tribe took his gold in trade for my body. It is said that giant flesh is not good to eat, anyway. Even orcs say this, and they will eat awful things. I once saw an orc begin eating an injured skunk while the animal still lived. If you try to discuss what is not fit for eating with an orc, it will be a short talk.

What was I saying? Ah, the time when I was dead. Yes. Let us go back to that. I lay there on the outskirts of the Ironspear village, poisoned and killed, soon to be eaten. My days of glory and might seemed to be over. However, the sorcerer had uses for me and performed his magic. From death, I returned, somehow getting to my feet and continuing when all others would have simply rotted. I remember none of this. No one living can now say exactly what words passed between the Ironspear and this wandering sorcerer. The nature of the dark spirits he called upon to return me to life are also lost to time.

When my mind and vision returned, I was walking through the swamp. Sorcerers have strange powers, and their magic is potent and impossible for a giant to understand. I found that I was no longer dead, and that I was a good distance away from the Ironspear village. I still felt very sick and could not feel my hands or feet. My head ached like I had been hit with a boulder. It is hard to return from death and involves pain. My tongue was swollen and I could not seem to move it to talk at first.

"See, Mungo. I have returned you to life. You owe me no less than a year and a day of servitude," the sorcerer said. I could tell his business because of his odd clothing and the smell of pungent spices around him. He moved his little hands in suspicious ways, like he was grabbing at things that were not visible. He had a shifty look about him. I didn't like him.

I thought about his words. It seemed that smashing him flat with my foot would be the best way, but that would have been rude, since he had restored life to my limbs. Also, I remembered my cousin Yaldag had killed a wizard once and had gone blind in one eye no more than a week later. Killing a sorcerer was probably bad luck, and my fortunes had already turned sour too often.

"Why have you done this, sorcerer? Why bring Mungo back from the dead?"

The human leaned against the trunk of a tree and put on a clever expression. "Because I have need of someone with your skills, and you would otherwise have been filling the orcs' bellies. Seems a waste."

"What do you want Mungo to do?"

"Oh, I shall think of something, I'm sure. There's always something that needs doing, and a pair of hands such as yours come in useful. Follow me."

"Who are you?" I asked.

"They call me Trachion. Trachion the Black."

I shook my head. "Your face is pale."

"Ah, but not my heart, Mungo. I'm a cruel and devious person. You had best remember that."

"All small folks are this way. Elf, Dwarf, Orc . . . they all have dark little hearts and are full of spite and meanness. They never let my kind alone and always wish to use us for some foul purpose. We giants have no friends among the small ones."

The sorcerer only smiled. "This is true. Know that I am worse than the rest, worse than the orcs who would have dined upon you. My word is good, though. Serve me for a year and a day, and you'll be free to go about your business, whatever that might be."

"Why would I want to work for you, if you are so bad?"

"Because bad people succeed. You've never succeeded at anything much in your life, have you? With me, you could."

His words confused me. "Talk sense!"

"You want to work with me because you'll be fed."

"What about wine and mead?"

"I'm sure we'll be able to find strong drink for you at times, as well. What do you say? I've already bought you, but I want you to feel like this is a fair business arrangement."

I thought about it, then spat on the ground and swore to follow the sorcerer.

It was my second big mistake of the week.

We walked for days into the mountains. It was a place that I did not know well. I think that the Greyshalks lived there somewhere, but we did not see them on that trip. I believe that it was because they feared me. They were right to do so, for I was strong in those days, and killed many with my club. Even now, when I am old and sick, I can kill an orc with a single blow most of the time. Then . . . then I was like great rocks falling from the mountains. None could stop me by force of arms. They could only hope to avoid my wrath.

As I walked, the sorcerer told me many things. I ignored them, mostly. At least his voice was not as annoying as little orcs, like the tricky No-Tusks who had killed me with his schemes. The thing I do remember is that he was obsessed with showing some other sorcerer that he was more mighty, that he had stronger magic. He talked of little else, save when he was saying bad things about my ability to think, or telling me to make preparations for camp, catch food, and the like.

I found him boring. He would not sing songs, play games, or tell tales of the old days, as we giants do when we are going on a long journey. No, he would whisper to himself and rub his hands together in a mean way, scheming. I tried to tell him how best to approach such a problem, but it was of little use.

"Kill this sorcerer. He will then know your power." These were my words. They seemed wise. Killing another warrior is an honored way of showing strength among men, orcs, and giants. I thought that it would probably do for magic folk, as well. He did not agree, and told me so at length.

"You are a foolish creature, Mungo. What can someone know when they are dead?"

I thought about this, having just been dead. It was true that I had not known much at that time. I didn't remember anything about being dead when I came back, either. The sorcerer had a point. I have always been accounted clever among giants, though, and was not ready to give up yet.

"Others would know. You would gain fame with magic wielders when they heard that you had destroyed a powerful sorcerer," I told him. "Reputation speaks with loud words, and others learn respect. This is what my grandsire, Bruug, said when he slew the lizard horror of Fire Mountain, and he spoke true words, for he was soon made chief." I did not mention that Bruug fell to drinking heavily and was soon deposed by Iardock Great-Arm and sent to live in the hinterland swamps. A giant doesn't speak ill of his kinsmen and forebears to outsiders, after all.

He shrugged, squinting up at me. "I don't care what others think. I want Varaldo to know my victory over him, and suffer with envy. I want to take from him all that he holds most dear, as he once did to me."

"You make things too complicated. When I am alive and my enemy is dead, that is enough. One who makes his vengeance a witch's brew will be the one forced to drink it in the end." I was quite proud of myself for that saying, which I had just made up on the spot, but Trachion, the sorcerer, had already fallen back into his waking fever dream of plans and plots, and never heard this great gem of wisdom as it came from my lips. I like to think it would have saved him great pain, perhaps saved us both a lot of difficulty later, but he was a stubborn and dense fellow. It may have done little good. Ah, well. The journey went on, and no powers of even the strongest wizard can go back and change things now.

The mountain valley was quiet when we arrived. Save for a few black-eyed ravens sitting on an old tree stump, there was but little life to be seen. By this time, it was full summer, so even the mountain valleys were warm at night and pleasant. At the far end of the little valley, a run-off river came from the snowfields above, and slowed to a narrow lake. I ignored Trachion's urgings that we get down to the business at hand and bounded off toward this lake. My mouth was parched and it had been a long time since I'd tasted truly clean water. My home in the swamp, at best, had brackish water that always tasted of rotting vegetation and mud.

My people, years and years ago, well before my grandsire's time, had been a mountain folk. None now live who know why we came down from the mountains and began living in the lowlands, near to the small folk with their schemes and malice. Perhaps we have angered the Mountain Gods and are being punished in exile now. It may be that the filthy Pyberian dwarves had something to do with it. At that moment, I was simply happy to be back where my people once came from, in a good, natural place with sweet water and a great number of tiny flowers growing across the meadow as the sun shined. It was the first time since I'd been dead that I really felt happiness again.

I pushed my face into the chill of the lake and drank deeply, splashing my hands into the water and brushing it back through my hair, which was like red, oiled straw by then.

When my face was clean and I had satisfied my thirst at last, I went back to the sorcerer, who stood impatiently, as if he could not have done something in my absence.

He held up a finger, his little face filled with anger. I could see the finger quiver with unspoken rage. "Make camp!" he finally shouted, then stomped away.

I said to myself then, "Mungo, this sorcerer is a crazy person."

Having given my word to help him for a year and a day, I had little choice but to keep doing so. Unlike the small folk, who are tricky and without honor, a giant will keep his word, even when things are not going well. I made camp.

The next morning, Trachion seemed to be in better spirits. The fact that I had been able to catch a large catfish and cook it for him had improved his mood. The more I traveled with him, the more it seemed that, despite having magical powers, Trachion was not very good at taking care of everyday matters, like getting food and finding his way. I sometimes wondered what he'd done before I was helping him. Bumbled along and gone hungry, I guess.

He directed me to a cave entrance on the far cliff wall, pointing to the darkness within. "There is an artifact of great power somewhere inside that cave. Go in there and find it for me, Mungo."

"What does it look like? How will I know when I find it?"

Trachion frowned. "You will know. If you cannot find it yourself, I'll follow when the way is clear."

I sat on my haunches. "Speak plainly, Sorcerer. Is there some menace down in that cave?"

He shifted from foot to foot and looked at me out of the corner of his eye. "There are stories. Perhaps there is a guardian."

"Some underground beast? Magic? What?" I was growing angry with him by this time.

"Likely it's just talk to keep people away. Whatever guarded the artifact is probably long since dead or has wandered of."

Looking at him, I did not trust his words. I was a

giant, after all. If it was merely a job to go and retrieve something, he could have hired a manservant. I went to the cave mouth and peered in, hands on hips.

The cave was not particularly large. I held back, scuffing the toe of my boot against the grass. Truth to tell, I have never really liked going into small spaces. They cause me to become nervous and lose my sense of direction. I have always been more of an outdoor giant. When I didn't respond, he frowned.

"Well? This is your first important labor for me, Mungo. Now, we see if my efforts at bringing you back from the spirit world were warranted or not."

I sighed. "How am I to see in the darkness of the cave?" I asked.

Trachion relented a bit. "Yes, I did forget that, didn't I? Bend down here and I'll fix that."

He took out a tub of strange, foul smelling paste and proceeded to paint something on my forehead. My whole face went numb while he did it, and I was unable to feel my lips or tongue. He had a distasteful look on his face when I began to drool all over the ground.

Trachion danced away, shaking some of my spittle off of his hand. "There. See that you don't rub it off, or the effect will be ruined."

"Whath ith it?" I said, my words distorted as if I were a drunkard.

"Why, I've drawn you another eye, an Obsidian Eye. It sees in the dark."

To be honest, I wondered if he'd gotten the spell wrong, for I was now feeling dizzy and strange all over. I went to hands and knees and entered the darkness of the cave, sloppily drooling all over my own hands, the ground, everything.

He had not lied, though. I could see through my normal two eyes, and the weak, waning light of the outside morning, but I could also see through the Obsidian Eye. This other vision was in colors and shadows that have no names in any tongue of giant or small folk. I couldn't just see the rocks, but into them, where the flecks of metal swam without moving. I looked down at my own hands, and I could see the spiderweb of bones inside the flesh. I didn't like it, and wanted it to be over as soon as possible. I wanted the whole year and a day to be over as quick as it could. It had only just begun, though. I would have berated myself for a fool, but my mouth, by this time, would make no useful word or sound, only releasing a torrent of spittle.

I do not know how many times I scraped my knees, or how often I bloodied my scalp against the roof of the cave as it grew smaller and smaller. Many, many times. I saw no magical artifact. I relied only on the weird vision Trachion had given me now, for there was no light at all in the deep part of the cave.

I crawled on, miserable and dizzy, half out of my mind with the spell of the Obsidian Eye. At last, the cave opened into a huge cavern. I was able to stand once again. Below, there was an underground lake that even the magic vision I had could not see across. I went to its shores and looked around. Back on my feet again and able to stand to my full height, without the stone pressing in around me, I didn't feel quite so bad. The effects of the magic, though, still hung on me like a weak poison. I walked on by the shores of the inky lake.

There, I found a place where the stone had been finished by hand. It was a shrine of some sort, I imagined. Resting upon the smooth stone was a large ball of metal, probably as heavy as a big human or a very fat dwarf. I picked it up and held it close to my face. I could tell that there were marks upon the globe, and that its outside casing was only a shell around some other substances within. With the Obsidian Eye, I tried to look at the deeper layers, but whatever magic the artifact was made from kept me from seeing anything but the surface.

At that time, something wet and slimy grasped my ankle and squeezed so hard that I shouted, dropping the globe, which fell directly on the large toe of my other foot. I shouted much louder. The foulest words in the giant language passed from my lips at that time, though they were so garbled by my numb tongue that they came out as utter nonsense.

I looked back toward the lake. Several tentacles came from there, each one as big around as a human's torso. The body of the creature that followed on in their wake shocked and disgusted me. I don't have the words to describe it, nor do I wish to.

In another moment, I was wrestling with the horror from the lake, its tentacles slapping on my skin, squeezing me with amazing strength. One of the tentacles wrapped around my face, its tip trying to invade my mouth. I tried to get my club free from my belt, but I couldn't. Doing the only thing I could, I grabbed on and squeezed back as hard as I could, trying to drag the creature further from the water.

That didn't work. With a sickening tug, I was pulled to the shore. A tentacle slapped at the tenderest of all spots on a male giant's body, and a pained noise burst from my mouth. Suddenly, I was in the water, the creature all around me, tentacles squirming and squeezing and trying to invade points that would bear no invasion.

As the water touched me, the Obsidian Eye washed away, and I was utterly blind.

I kicked and punched, squeezed and pulled and bit and screamed in long streams of bubbles beneath the ink-dark water. I don't know how long I was down below its surface, or how, exactly, I prevailed, but I did. By feel alone, I found my way to the shore once again and collapsed, covered in the jellied innards of the lake horror, pain filling every joint and muscle. I could not rise. Stranded and unable to see my way toward escape, I passed out.

Trachion came later, and I was able to roll the ball of metal out of the cave. He sat there in the lean-to I made and studied it for three days, while I took several baths in the lake to try and get the awful monster jelly off of me. I was also made lame by the fact that my stones had swollen to twice their normal size, and filled the pit of my stomach with pain. I lay there, waist deep in the cold water, feeling bad for myself, almost wishing that the Ironspear tribe had eaten me and made an end to my misfortunes.

My pain subsided, though, and I regained my enjoyment of the mountains. By the time Trachion finally gave up on trying to figure out the magic of the metal ball, I was myself again, and realized that things were not so bad. I had, after all, bested a mysterious creature from deep underground with only my bare hands. It was a deed of a great giant hero, after all. In the stories, it is always the deed that is spoken of, not of the pain and doubt and swollen stones afterward. I tried to fool myself into thinking that working with the sorcerer was all to the good, that I would find further impressive deeds along the way, and would become the giant I had always hoped for as a result. I was young, after all, and very foolish.

One morning, I woke to see Trachion rolling the metal ball up the hill. I thought that it was good for him to do something for himself, and so I didn't offer to help or let him know that I had awakened. I saw him push the ball over the rough scrabble at the cave entrance and let it go. I could hear the sound of it rolling and smashing against walls as it went down the heavily slanted tunnel and out of sight.

"Done with the artifact?" I asked as the sorcerer returned, out of breath and sweaty on the forehead.

He gave me a sour expression. "Never mind that. Let's get moving."

"What does it do?" I asked. "Why go into that hellish cave?"

"Too many questions!"

I folded my arms. I did his bidding, but I was more than twice his height and could pick him up with one hand. "Tell me why, or I am going to stay here until tomorrow."

Trachion hopped from foot to foot, as angry as I'd yet seen him. For a time, words failed him, and the veins in his temples throbbed. I thought that he would fall in a faint. Finally, he gathered himself. "You see . . . "

I waited. He began to speak a few times, then stopped. I didn't think it was a hard question. I considered dropping the issue, waiting for nightfall, and sneaking away. At last, the words came to him.

"Varaldo has many magical artifacts. They increase his power. If I hope to defeat him, I will need to have potent items to augment my own magic. I hoped to understand the secret of that metal sphere, but I could get nothing from it." He looked downcast.

"Not all adventures are successful." I told him. "I'll go now."

"Let us move, then," he said, regaining his assured attitude.

And move we did. We went back down to the foothills and went south along the verge of the mountains for several days, until I knew we were in the terrain where giants had once lived, our old homeland. It was not long after that I saw a giant house built atop a crag in the distance. You can always tell a giant house, for we are builders without peer. We are not afraid of using much lumber and even more tar to fill the cracks.

Giant houses are superior to all others.

"There is a giantess who lives in the house up there. Her name is Rhalda. Go up there and convince her that she should give you the Baldrick of Lechmar. It's said that she wears it as a bracelet or armband of some kind. Do what must be done to make sure that she gives it up."

These were my orders. I knew dread in my heart then, for all of you are aware of how potent and angry a giantess can be, and how their hearts are filled with fire and wrath. I did what I could do to make myself presentable. I spent most of the day in the woods, hunting. After I was able to catch two wild hogs and press them to butter in a sack, I finally dared to approach her dwelling.

The appropriate twenty paces from Rhalda's door, I announced myself. "Rhalda, I am Mungo, son of Mogo, son of Bruug. I have come to your door bearing a gift, and hope you will speak to me."

Rhalda appeared then. She was great of hip and bosom, and had strong, fleshy arms. She squinted at me. Rhalda was very tall for a giantess, almost equal to my own height. In those days, when I was a lean young giant, she probably outweighed me by the measure of a pony.

"You're one of Bruug's get?" she asked, a half-grin showing that she still had most of her teeth. "I knew him, back in the old days. He was a great buffoon. It's known that his whole line are nose-pickers and imbeciles. Why would I wish to see anyone of that ilk?"

I felt my face flush. "I don't know, but I do know

this. If I had known you were such a hag, with a sharp tongue and dull wits, I wouldn't have brought these two pressed boars as a gift. I'm of half a mind to eat them myself, right in sight of your hovel here, which is built as poorly as a human structure."

"Filthy stripling!" she shouted, launching herself toward me. She was of such a girth that seeing her begin to jog was rather spectacular, with elements of her flesh moving in any number of directions as she pressed forward. I began to laugh despite myself, but that was brought to a halt as she punched me in the eye, causing a shower of sparks and falling stars to shoot across my brain.

We were tussling then, she trying to gouge at my eyes, and kick me in the feet and shins. I bit down hard upon one of her shoulders. Rhalda got one of her feet behind my heel, and we both tumbled to the dirt, wrestling and rolling back and forth for a good long time. She nearly bit my thumb off, but I was able to punch her in the ear to dislodge the digit from her mouth.

As night fell, we both lay on our backs, out of breath and exhausted, the tussle concluded, our voices now hitching into laughter.

"You are not so bad for a git of moronic Bruug," she admitted.

"And for an old crone giantess who has grown too fat and mean, I find that I like you well, Rhalda," I said.

She took me inside her dwelling and we shared the pressed boar. She had a cask of mead. We became drunk and we wrestled again. This bout was not so rough as the first, but it went on for most of the night.

Just as dawn began at the far horizon, I was able to shake loose from her grapple and ease the item I'd been sent for from her fleshy wrist. I returned again to the sorcerer, exhausted, with two blackened eyes, a swollen thumb, and sundry other wounds. Still, I had been victorious, and held a sense of pride in my heart. Was there a pang for stealing away with Rhalda's bracelet? Perhaps, but I knew that, had the stations been reversed, she would have stolen from me without remorse.

The sorcerer sniffed at the magical item, made a face, then washed it in a stream for a long time. When it had dried, he put it across one shoulder and stood there, waiting for something to happen. Nothing seemed to. He whispered a great many angry words to himself and then demanded that we move along.

"Nothing?" I asked.

He shook his head. "Perhaps the magic has been worn off, likely by foul giant sweat." He did not remove the baldric, though. It seemed to me that Trachion had poor luck with magic items.

"Where are we going now?"

"We have to go into the city."

"They don't allow giants into the city. I'll be fighting the whole city guard if we try," I told him.

Trachion looked angry. He often did. I think that his basic problem was that he had never learned to be happy about anything. He always fought against what was so hard that he couldn't enjoy the good things about every day. Magic folk are fools in this way.

"Very well, I'll take you to the edge of the Fey Glade, and you'll wait there for me. There, at least, you'll have a hard time getting yourself in trouble."

I shrugged and followed him. I never remember getting myself in trouble. I am always sensible and do the wise thing. It is only when I get talked into helping other people that things go wrong. There was no sense in debating this with the sorcerer. The only voice he really heard was his own. I hoped, as foolish as he was, that he would meet his demise in the city, leaving me free of his schemes and plots. All of them led to my discomfort and seemed to accomplish little good for him. For Trachion, it would be good to be dead, so that he wouldn't know things and want things any more.

I had not been to a Fey Glade before. I stood there, very still, after Trachion left to do his business in the nearby city. My impression was that the Fey Glade was much like any other forest, only more so. Where there were normally bright clearings with twittering birds, there were many bright clearings with an overabundance of birds that set the ear reeling with songs and sounds. Where there would normally have been a few darkened nooks where the temperature seemed too cold and some odd shiver climbed up a lone wanderer's spine, there were dark and forbidding expanses of wood where it seemed perilous to tread.

The best idea was to simply wait and do as little as possible. I sat in one of the clearings, meadow birds of all sizes and colors flitting around, trying to make nests in my ears, pecking leftovers of previous dinners from my shirt front, and generally making themselves pests. I shooed them away, but they were not afraid of me. Fey birds. They make me tired, just thinking of them.

I soon got hungry and thirsty, as well as annoyed by the noise and bother of the birds. Try as I could, I was not able to just stay put. In the search for a good stream to drink from, and possibly fish, I wandered into one of the dark and forbidding parts of the forest. I could feel unknown things watching me from behind bushes and up in the high branches of the trees. A squirrel raced back and forth on the limb of a tree, its little eyes full of rage. It seemed almost to shake its tiny fist at me and yell curses.

Of course, squirrels are this way in all forests, so at least that was comforting. The feeling of being watched by unseen eyes was not. I managed to find a stream, but the idea of staging a true hunt in such a wood seemed perilous at best. I drank my fill and resigned myself to going hungry. I had done it many times before, and giants are adept at a fast. We often must go for many days without food, and we must eat far less than a human would, weight for weight.

This doesn't mean that going without is comfortable. The sun was beginning to wane behind the trees, and I found my way back to the clearing where I had started. I thought it was the clearing anyway. I hadn't remembered the stone obelisk in the corner from the previous time. It was a clearing, one way or another, and would have to do.

I held my empty belly and lay down on the grass. The evening birds swooped and dived over my head in the twilight, giving me no peace at all. Even so, I closed my eyes and tried to rest. Sleep would at least take the hunger away for a while, passing the time until the sorcerer would return and lead me on the next foolish venture.

I awoke to music. The sounds of flutes and harps, of lyres and lutes. Over all of it, the sweet sound of female voices, singing in wordless harmony. I sat up and rubbed my eyes. All around me, the Fey creatures danced and frolicked. There were women with the bodies of deer. There were squat, stunted little sprites. There were dim-eyed creatures that looked like small hounds that had taken up walking on their hind legs, dancing around and playing their tiny drums.

They smiled at me and danced around me. I found that I was at the center of a wide circle of torches held on stands. The Fey creatures were having some moon festival all around the clearing. Their music, while merry on the surface and with the rhythms that make you wish to dance, had something darker underneath, as if somewhere within the honey notes was a hint of venom, a touch of danger.

I rose to try and find another place to sleep, but they hemmed me in, dancing around my feet, grasping onto my legs, holding up plates of food for me to eat. In all of this, they never said a word I could understand, but only beckoned, danced, and smiled.

Seated again, I took their food. I was so very hungry, after all, and they seemed kind enough. They brought me tubers from the ground, tender mushrooms, sweet honeycomb, and a dozen loaves of bread. With each treat, they brought their largest cup of honey wine. It was sweet and potent, and made my head swim, but I took it nonetheless. Giants of my line have a weakness for strong drink, going back to Bruug and before. While we are sensible and wise in most cases, we will often do foolish things when we are in our cups.

Soon, I was full of their food and deeply drunk. My eyes hooded and I could do nothing but let sleep take me. As I lay there, not quite passed out, but unable to open an eye for the drink and food in my system, I could feel something begin to happen, but I couldn't tell what it was. A tickling feeling spread throughout me. I wanted to care, wanted to find out what was happening, but I was too weary from the strong drink.

It was only later that I would learn the truth, and know the foul reason why they had pretended kindness.

Something hit me in the head. I could feel my brain rattle around inside my skull like a walnut inside a jar. It hurt a great deal. I tried to rise, but found that my body wouldn't move at all. I couldn't open my eyes. I wondered if I was dead again, and hoped that I wasn't. Trachion would likely lose patience with me and get himself another giant if I kept getting myself killed.

Sorcerers like him are not patient and forgive only their own failures.

After a moment I suffered another shock, like someone was hitting me with a large hammer, right in the middle of the forehead. My eyes popped open at last, and I found that was exactly what was happening.

A type of Fey creature with a goat's horns and furry belly, but the face of an angry human was hitting me again and again with a wooden sledge he swung with two hairy hands. I saw the hammer come downward and tried to flinch away, but nothing happened but the feel of my hair pulling taut. The sledge fell just over my left eye, hard enough to cause bursts of color through my vision and the sound of a hollow log being hit with a stick.

I gave out a yell. He yelled back at me and hit me in the head again. I tried to get up, but something was wrong, I could feel my limbs, knew they were straining against something, but I couldn't move them. I shook my head, and the hammer-swinger jumped back, likely afraid that I would bite him. I could just see the edge of my shoulder, how the revelers had braided me into the grass with careful stitching. Sod hung in clumps from where the grass had been twined into my hair, and blood dripped into my eyes.

While I craned my head, the furry hammer-swinger hit me right on the ear with his sledge. The pain shot through me like I'd had a spike driven in there. I surged harder than I had before, and I felt their stitching break. Roaring, I tore free of the ground and jumped to my feet.

The other Fey creatures stood at the verge of the clearing, watching me with their glowing eyes. A handful of the furry goatmen rushed forward with clubs and hammers, hitting me in the legs and thighs. I kicked at one of them and just missed. Another, I managed to stomp to jelly into the ground. A fourth hit me right on the point of the knee, raising a howl to my lips. I reached down and grabbed him, pulling one of his arms off and throwing him into the forest.

This caused a general panic in the Fey creatures. Several of them shot spells at me that caused my vision to go all wrong and my balance to leave me. I stumbled around the clearing, half blind and limping, as they made their retreat.

I found myself suddenly alone in the Fey Glade, shouting at them, still drunk and now hung over, my head covered with lumps and fresh bruises, my knee seized up from the injury. I didn't know which way to go, which direction would take me to safety, so I sat in the center of the clearing and watched the fire burn low and turn to embers, feeling sorry for myself.

It was difficult to stay awake and alert until morning, but I knew that, should I sleep again, they would use all their powers to kill me. Once again, through no fault of my own, I served as a victim for the small folks' schemes and evil.

By the time the sorcerer came back two days later, I was so exhausted and ill that it was all I could do to follow him upon the trail. He hardly seemed to notice, consumed as he was with something that he had learned in the city.

"Now Varaldo will see," he kept saying.

"What will he see?"

This time, Trachion was happy enough to talk. "I will show him that he should have never left me behind, never dismissed me as a second rate sorcerer."

I raised one eyebrow. "I thought that you were angry at him because he stole your woman or tricked you out of treasure." These, of course, were the time-honored reasons for seeking vengeance.

Trachion sighed. "As if sorcerers would fight over such petty things. No, we were once partners, the best of friends. Through luck, he always seemed to grow more noteworthy, his legend growing. Soon, it was as if we had never known one another; as if I wasn't his equal in magic, his oldest friend. He cast me adrift in the world. He . . . "

The sorcerer's chin quivered. I thought he might be on the verge of tears. I had been betrayed by a lot of people in my life, but never by a friend. Then again, I never really had a friend. For a moment, I almost felt bad for him. This, though, was a terrible reason for revenge. Perhaps it was not his fault. Some people have no knack for these things.

We went away on our next journey, and I was glad to leave the Fey Glade behind. In all my days, I have never gone back. Giants are wise enough to avoid such places, once they know how dangerous they are. I didn't try to sway Trachion from his quest, as I knew it would do no good. He was not in his right mind, and his heart was hurt. It is hard to speak sense to such people.

I was hesitant to go onto the plains of Serrin, as there are many humans there, and they will almost always attack a giant on sight. The sorcerer insisted, and he said that this place had long since been abandoned by all but the rare lunatic wanderer or outcast.

"Very well, but if I have to kill many of your kinsman, don't say that I didn't warn you about this."

Trachion shrugged. "Kill whomever you like. I live only for myself, and for the day when Varaldo will learn of his doom at my hands."

I thought that wasn't much to live for. He had problems in his head, and they would not be solved while he lived and breathed. I felt pity for him, and hoped that his death would soon come to pass, so that he would know peace and I would know freedom. To speak truly, I was more interested in my freedom than anything. Being a servant had begun to weigh heavily on my mind and I missed my home in the bog.

We came to a long, flat place, where someone had stacked a ring of stones long ago. The grass had grown up high around them for years and I could see moss and lichen growing on the rocks where they stood. The rocks were huge, and were from the far away mountains.

"Giants built this place," I told Trachion.

"Maybe. Maybe clever men with great magic. Maybe a race that all whispers of are now lost. It is not important. There is magic in these stones, and I can use it to transport us far away."

"How?"

Trachion pursed his lips and made a dismissive gesture. "I have no time to try and teach a dolt like you the fine points of sorcery! Just . . . stand over there and don't touch anything."

I saw that the lichen on the stones was the kind that tasted good, but Trachion caught me and forbade me to lick the standing stones. I thought, and not for the first time, that he made it very difficult to have any fun.

It was often hard for me to tell whether Trachion was performing a magical spell or just muttering to himself. He was such a surly little man that his angry whispers to himself or some person who was not nearby happened at every hour of the day.

While he prepared the magic to make us travel to some far-off land, I found a comfortable place to sit on the grass and did my best to repair the holes in my boots. Giants, since they can rarely rely on anyone else to help them, have to be good at many things. I am sad to say that I was never much good at mending things, but that didn't keep me from trying when I had to.

From time to time, I would look up from my needle and thread to see Trachion toiling at his magic. He used a stone dish and a stirring rod of some kind to combine all sorts of herbs and powders from his bags. He then added them to a small pot over a fire he'd asked me to build.

This task, of course, had come at a bad time, so I had to hop around on one foot to try and keep my stocking out of the wetness of the grass. As I had come to expect from him, Trachion heaped insults upon my head. I believe that all the meanness in him came from the fact that he did not believe in his own worth, and his only joy was to make others sad. That, or he just did not like me. In the end, it didn't matter.

Foul smoke arose from the mixture that the sorcerer boiled. I moved to stay upwind of the worst of it, but there was no way to escape the awful smell. He then stripped to the waist and painted a symbol on his chest with what looked to be his own waste. I sat there, my eyes burning, wondering if there was a good way to slip away from the sorcerer. Was it too late to stomp him to jelly? How much more of the year remained? My spirits were low, and I almost surrendered to hopelessness.

The sorcerer finished his incantations at last and sickly orange light hung around all the standing stones. He approached, haggard and out of breath. He smelled terrible, worse than rotten chicken, even.

"Quickly, now," he urged. "To the center of the stones!"

I didn't wish to stand near him, but I slid my boot on and followed him. When we got there, he began to make noises that seemed like the barking of a sick dog. This went on for some time, with him leaping and twisting his body in a random, painful-looking way. The merciful course seemed to be to just put the poor man out of his misery, but I was still concerned that killing him would be bad luck. Besides, he had caused me enough distress by then that I had little mercy left for him.

The sun set, and his antics continued in the darkness. The level of orange flame that hung around the standing stones became greater, until each one blazed like a hot campfire. I was footsore from standing there so long, and my back ached. I yawned. I didn't believe that anything would happen.

Something did. Bolts of orange fire burst from all the standing stones, lancing toward us. I was certain that we'd be burned to a cinder. Ducking, I covered my head just as the bolts hit us. My skin burst into flames. I screamed. My body was ripped asunder, and I knew no more.

How long was I dead that time? I cannot say. Who brought Trachion and I back from the dead? It could only have been the gods, for they were not done with me yet. I still had a great destiny to fulfill. That must have been it. The gods know of these things, of what must be, and who must live or die. For those few, death is not always the end. I will not tell you to hope for such things, for just as the gods may save you, they may also cut you down at any moment or steer the road of your life onto the most difficult of paths. Take it from me, one who has known their mercy and their wrath.

We were sprawled in a dusty square in the land called Aten, when our limbs knitted back together and life returned to our hearts. I was sore all over, and my vision was all wrong. I stood up, and quickly fell on my face. I threw up all over Trachion. He began to rail at me, but then began throwing up himself. The pains of our coming back to life kept on for much of the night, and we were forlorn as the morning dawned.

After we'd managed to clean up as best we could near the one working cistern, we began to explore the abandoned city. The day grew hot. I had a lot of time to look around while I trailed after the sorcerer. Far off to the west, there was a line of red bluffs. In all other directions, there were only waves of yellow sand. Though we saw no one, I thought that the city was too well kept to be empty.

Trachion was unaware of everything, though, rummaging through old buildings and digging in places where the sand had piled high near the city's many places of worship to their unknown gods.

We searched for most of the day before the sorcerer finally found what he was looking for. It was a small metal rod with runes all over it and a head made of gold and blue gems. It looked valuable, the sort of thing that smart people sell to a jewelry vendor. Trachion fell to his knees and held the scepter like he had just found a toy from boyhood.

I sighed, and the sorcerer looked up at me, his eyes angry. "I would not expect you to understand this, Mungo, but this . . . this artifact is one of the most powerful magical items of this ancient people. While they are long gone, this will finally allow me to defeat the foul Varaldo!"

"I think people still live here," I said.

"Nonsense! This place has been deserted for an eon."

It would not be too long before he would learn better.

Trachion began walking back the way we'd come, sure of his course and without a clue about the danger we were in. I felt eyes upon us and knew that the artifact he'd taken from the ancient structure would get us into trouble, but what could I do? The sorcerer was a fool, perhaps a madman, and I had agreed to help him with his lunatic wanderings.

I made sure that my club was at the ready, riding easy from the strap against my hip. There was no question in my mind that I would have need of it. I had been wrong before, but it is always better to be on guard. A giant's instincts and cunning are his most important tools. Our size, brawn, and wisdom are what we're known for, but strength is of little use to fools, and smarts, as Trachion himself showed, are not always helpful.

Like a wolf on the hunt, I moved forward, noticing everything, hearing every sigh of the wind. The foul odor of Trachion's earlier spell still hung about his shoulders, so that was all I could smell, and he was in the midst of a long rant about the many ways he would torment his enemy and bring him low. That did, I fear, make it more difficult to concentrate after a while. Once again, I thought of the benefit to the world and myself if I simply raised a foot and stomped upon him, ending his miserable existence. My only concern was that I was not sure where we were at the time or how to get back home. At this point, I was almost willing to brave the bad luck that one gets for killing a wizard. If I came away only blind in one eye or with a permanent limp, I was willing to make that sacrifice.

While I stalked forward, murder on my mind, the enemy moved to hem us in. I believe in my heart that they were invisible and perfectly silent all that time. I have heard tales of certain creatures who can turn themselves to stone and wait a hundred years for something to happen, then leap into life and flesh again at a moment's notice. Something much like that happened in that city in the desert. It was only my experienced hunter's eye and my giant cunning that knew we were in danger.

When we were back to the dusty square where we'd first sprawled, dead and awaiting the kindness of the gods to return life to our hearts, the enemy appeared, surrounding us on all sides.

They were short little women with brown arms and sand colored kilts to cover them. They had the heads of hawks, and each of them wore a medallion of bronze with a beetle of some sort engraved on it. Of greater importance, they all held swords with forward-curving sickles on the end of them, their hawk eyes glaring at us with a killing light.

One of them, with a hawk head that had flecks of white feathers upon the sides of her face, came forward and pointed. "You cannot remove the sacred scepter of the old goddess from this place!"

She said the name of the god, but it made no sense to me, and I couldn't pronounce it for all the mead the Beyklans could brew in a year, let alone remember it after all this time.

Trachion turned to me and cowered. This was a new development, and it took a minute for me to see what he was up to.

"Mercy! Please, have mercy on me! I am a simple servant, and this evil giant has forced me to come here and steal your relics. Every night and day, he threatens to kill me and make a wind chime from my bones. It is he who devised this plan. He is your enemy!"

With that, the betraying sorcerer ran with surprising speed and leaped through the door of one of the old buildings, leaving me alone with a dozen of the hawk-headed warrior women, who looked even angrier than they had a moment before.

"Bastard!" I shouted as Trachion disappeared. I pulled free my club and rushed the hawk women before me, smashing two of them before they had a chance to do more than yell their battle cries.

Though I'd known Trachion was a bit of a madman and that he valued my judgment about as much as dog droppings, I had thought the man at least had a certain honor about him. That often goes along with vengeance. Those who have flexible ethics, often as not, will only claim vengeance upon those who are easy pickings. At that time, there was still some hope in my heart that there were a few good small people. Other than the kindly Blue Lip tribe of orcs, I was never to find any that could be trusted.

I went to work then, using the lessons I had learned hard and suffered scars to gain. There is an art to fighting small people. The first rule is that you can never stand still and let them surround you. There are big veins in the feet and legs, and the ones with spears will try to stab you in the stones if you let them.

No, a giant has to keep moving, keep breaking holes in their circle of fighters, if he wants to survive. I found an old ruin and fought with my back to the building, swinging wild strokes to keep them from getting too close. They were quick though, and I was bleeding from ten places before I was able to smash another one of the hawk people with my club.

Unlike the average angry peasant, they were not disheartened as their friends were smashed to pulp by my mighty attacks. No, these were true warriors, and they would not quit so easily.

Sweat and blood ran free from my skin. The breath in my lungs burned, and the speed of my club's strikes began to slow. They were good fighters and knew that a giant's energy will ebb if the fight is long enough. I smashed one more, breaking the woman's back, so that she writhed and groaned on the sandy paving stones while her sisters dashed forward and cut another bleeding gash in my thigh.

Trachion chose this moment to make his appearance once more. He stood on the side street, to the left of the hawk warriors. I could only see him because I was tall enough to see over the corner of the building. He shouted out a spell and a noise as loud as close thunder rolled across the ancient city. It hurt my ears, even though I was not directly in line with its blast.

The hawk women, however, were. They fell to the ground, dropping their weapons and holding their hands against the sides of their hawk heads. They were strange creatures, able to change their forms, because a few of them yanked the hawk faces off, revealing human faces below.

This knowledge offended me, and I could do nothing but smash them to gristle on the ground as they took themselves apart and lay reeling from Trachion's magic. In a moment, there were only a few warriors left, the ones who had suffered a lesser thunder blast than the others. Seeing that their fight was lost and staying would only cause their doom, they disappeared into the mysterious places within the ruined city. We did not see them again.

I pointed my club at the sorcerer. "You are not to be trusted."

He raised an eyebrow. "Of course not. It doesn't matter. We have what we came for, and it should happen any time now."

"What should—" I began to ask. It was at that moment that my vision flooded with orange light. We were again scalded and torn limb from limb by the magic that moves great distances.

I had become very tired of coming back from death. Each time, it seemed worse. At the time, I believed that I had offended the gods somehow, and that they would never allow me to die, but only curse me to walk the earth for ages, suffering every torment and privation imaginable for lifetime after lifetime. I was young then and all my setbacks felt very personal. It is only with age that we realize that whatever happens to us is part of a greater puzzle and that the gods and unknown forces have plans for us. Often, what seems like cruelty to us is only resolve on their part. They knew, for instance, that I was sturdy enough of heart to suffer these tortures and remain myself. They knew I would never give up, never go mad, like unfortunate Trachion.

It took us a few days of rest to feel well enough to travel again. The sickness of returning to life was compounded by all the wounds I'd taken in the fight. Trachion's cowardly dash to safety had resulted in his turning an ankle, which became swollen and purple with bruises. I said nothing, but I was well pleased that he had taken this injury.

We said little to each other. I nursed a grudge.

"I knew you could handle yourself, Mungo. You have a reputation as a great fighter. It was a gamble on my part, but I needed them to bunch together, and I needed time to prepare my incantation. It worked perfectly, don't you think?"

I pushed my lips together. I think he only came back because things looked favorable, and he wanted me with him for the next part of the journey, but I reluctantly accepted his story. Much of the year was now gone, for there were many boring journeys I have spared you during my telling of the tale. I resolved to try and complete the year. After that, I would stay well clear of all magic folk for the rest of my days. It was an oath to myself that I would be doomed to break, of course. One day, I will speak of what happened when I met the Five Witches, but that is for another time.

The sorcerer Varaldo lived atop a rock outcropping that looked like a short set of stairs. His house, built of stone with a wooden roof, was big and well kept. There was a stable nearby, and some buildings where it looked like his servants lived, as well as those who cared for the farmland nearby. It looked like a good place to live, and spoke of both wealth and power. Looking at Trachion, I saw a ragged man with worn-out boots and a dusty robe, a man I had never seen with a single gold coin in hand.

"This is your enemy's land?"

Trachion told me that it was. "The fruit of all his ill-gotten wealth. Much of this should be mine. Had he not been given all the luck in the world, I would have an estate just this grand."

I remembered the old giant proverb then. "He who has the mightiest arm and the swiftest club will often find himself lucky."

When Trachion didn't respond to my wisdom, I continued. "Well, if we are to bring him ruin, we should think of a plan. Rob his servants and kill them when they are alone. Burn down his barn in the night. What any clever fighter would do."

The sorcerer shook his head. "No, no. This is a

duel between the greatest living sorcerers, not some petty skirmish."

If Trachion was one of the greatest sorcerers in the world, they were a weedy and questionable group, I thought to myself. I shrugged and was soon told to make camp for the night.

"We should at least come at him in the night, when he may be drunk and weary," I told him. His ears would not hear my words.

Trachion insisted that we come to the place in the light of day. Because of this, Varaldo's servants were able to warn him of our arrival well in advance. By the time we were in front of his mansion, he had an array of armored warriors at his back and several held longbows with deadly arrows fitted to their strings.

Varaldo was an older human, with his graying hair missing in a large horseshoe pattern at the top of his head. He had missed no meals, judging by his fat belly, and wore fine clothes. His hands were held easy at his hips as he watched us come closer.

"I have heard rumors of you lately, my friend. They said that you had a giant working for you, but I didn't believe it. How have you been, Trachion?" Varaldo's voice was soothing, his face friendly. It would have been a grave mistake to think that he was harmless, though. I always make it a point to be on guard with small folk who are not frightened of me.

"You know how I have been all these years, Varaldo," Trachion growled. His eyes flashed with rage.

Varaldo made a slight shrug. "How could I? I have not talked with you for half a lifetime, my friend. Not since . . . well, since that unfortunate misunderstanding when we were hardly more than boys. I have always felt bad about that, you should know. I wished to apologize for my part in the matter, but you were nowhere to be found. Now, perhaps, we can mend things between us and be partners again, like the way things were before."

Trachion's body shook with his anger. Varaldo's men saw it and tensed. Mailed hands reached for swords all around, and one of the archers whispered strange words as he and his men aimed their arrows at me. I knew they would not miss and arrows enchanted with magic would be worse than any others that had pierced my hide. I loosened my club at my belt and rolled my shoulders. Varaldo's men would give me the fight of my life.

"Gentlemen, please. We wish to avoid any unnecessary troubles." Varaldo made a calming gesture. I had stepped away from Trachion now. My pledge had been to help him in his journey, not to get involved with a duel between wizards.

Trachion calmed himself, forcing a smile that held more madness than mirth. "Perhaps you are right, Varaldo. It is time, after all these years, to put things right between us." He slowly pulled out the scepter we'd found in the desert city, holding it before him.

"What have you got there, Trachion?" Varaldo asked.

"This? Nothing much, just the tool I'll use to defeat you." With that, Trachion swept the scepter across his body and shouted something in the language of magic. All of Varaldo's warriors slumped to the ground, unmoving. Varaldo himself was unharmed.

"Interesting. You've put my henchmen to sleep, but I think you'll find that I'm capable of dealing with you and your giant without any assistance. I always have been more than a match for you in sorcery, my friend. If you must know, I only carried on pretending friendship to you as long as I did because you were an entertainment, an unwitting jester that amused me. When you imagined that we would be equals, true partners, I could countenance you no longer. I had to see you ruined. I see now that I was right to have done so."

The sudden cruelty in his voice was surprising. Varaldo pulled forth a bent stick from up one of his sleeves, holding it easily in his hand.

Trachion pointed the scepter at his great enemy. "You don't know what I have here, Varaldo. This artifact has the power to defeat you ten times over, to rain a curse of fire from the sky. That is not what I'll do to you this day, however. No, I want you to live, and to suffer for what you did to me!"

Trachion yelled something, and a bolt of shimmering energy burst from the scepter. At the same time, Varaldo performed a spell of some kind and pointed the bent stick in his hand. A flash and the crack of a giant boulder splitting in two filled the air. I blinked my eyes, blinded for a second.

Both men were still there, still upright and healthy enough. Trachion grinned, shaking his fist. "Now, you will walk the world in shame, suffering all the worst treatment that men and monsters will see fit to give you. I have stolen your magic and made you no more than a peasant in fine clothing, while I will be the greatest sorcerer this land has yet known."

Trachion let out a whoop and jumped from foot to foot.

Varaldo waited until this celebration was complete, his face guarded, his hands folded before him.

"What do you have to say now that I have given you ultimate defeat? Am I a jester, a diversion to you, now that you've been brought low?" Trachion asked.

Varaldo took a breath and let it out. "What do I have to say?" He smiled. "You got the spell wrong, you nitwit. It is I who possess all of *your* magic to augment my own, not the reverse. You've overreached once again. This time, far worse than ever before. You were once an eager bumbler, but the years have been unkind. You are a madman who listens to his own maniacal whispers in the night. Now, at least, the paltry magic that was yours is in safer hands."

"No . . . it couldn't be." Trachion looked down at his hands like they were unknown to him, someone else's. "Not my magic . . . "

He looked back to where I stood. "Mungo! You must save me now!" The sound of his squealing voice revolted me.

I spat on the ground. "I agreed to help you. I did. I fought creatures and went to strange lands with you. I put up with your mean words and your lunatic behavior. I never said that I would fight your wizard duels for you." I shook my head. "No, you are alone in this Trachion. My service to you ends now."

The sorcerer turned back to his great enemy, who

smiled calmly.

"Alone and outmatched," Varaldo said. He swept his crooked stick across the air, and a hundred spiders made from fire appeared at his feet, each one as large as a plump rat. They swarmed on the grass, crawling over each other in their numbers, rushing forward with a noise that made my skin crawl and itch.

Trachion screamed and began to run. The spiders of flame were faster, and soon caught up. The whole place filled with his screaming and the smell of burning hair. I was not happy, but I felt no great sadness for the man, either. It was better that he was dead and I was free. I believe that the gods wanted me to learn from his mistakes. Vengeance is a tough and rotten meat to survive on. There are better things to consider, more fruitful roads to walk.

Varaldo, the other sorcerer, came nearer to me now. His men had begun to wake up, and were sitting on the ground, shaking their heads to improve their vision.

"What shall become of you now, Giant? Your master is dead, his quest a failure."

"His quest was not mine. I only came along because he brought me back from death," I told him. "I offered the man good advice, but he wouldn't listen."

"Brought you back from death, did he?" Varaldo did not seem to believe that Trachion could do such things, but I knew he could. Despite his failings as a man and as a sorcerer, he had potent magic.

I nodded. "My debt to him is paid now. I will go back where I lived before, though it is a long journey."

"Trachion was not the easiest person to get along with."

"No. He was mean as an old donkey. I can see why you cast him aside."

"He must have seen some utility in your presence, to have kept you around." Varaldo stroked his chin. He had a way of talking that made you wonder what he would say next, and if the conversation would ever be over. Men like him can pet a snake and not be bitten. They are dangerous.

"I was valuable to him. It was only my aid and guidance that brought him here. He would have starved or become lost in the wilderness otherwise," I told Varaldo.

"Perhaps, if you're not altogether soured on the prospect, you might work for me. I think you'd find that I'm a much more reasonable man. Now, with Trachion's powers added to my own, I may well be among the most powerful sorcerers in all the world. There'd be gold and fame in it for you."

On some other day, it would have been tempting. If he'd offered a week later, when I was hungry and lost in a forest, my club cracked in half, one boot filled with brackish water, I would surely have taken him up on his offer. That day, though, all I wanted to do was to get away from everyone who made magic and make my own way in the world.

"With the power you have, you won't need me," I said. "It is time I go home, unless you would try to stop me." I put my hand on the club, just to show him that I would not be his pet.

Varaldo shrugged. "The offer stands. If you change your mind, return to me here. Arrangements could be made. You could taste fame and know riches in your day, Mungo."

Later, I did change my mind, but I would never return to him, for other things would come about. I was bound to have the adventures that have become legend, to save the Blue Lip tribe and dare the curses of the Five Witches. I would gain fame by my own hand and live to be the fat, sick, old creature you see today.

On that day, so long ago, a young giant in the peak of his powers walked away from the offers and bribes of the sorcerer, his steps quick, his back straight and square, his heart yearning for home. Though he was weary from the road and far from all he knew, he had proven himself mighty. Death's hand could not claim him, for he was Mungo the Undying.

MUNGO THE UNDYING

Varaldo the Great became one of the most powerful sorcerers in the world, and he and his men were called upon to defend the realm against invaders many times.

Read the next story, "Unerring" by Patrick S. Tomlinson, to learn the fate of one of Varaldo's most powerful spell-archers.

Unerring
by Patrick S. Tomlinson

Through gossamer green threads of magic, my master's life-force flowed from his fingertips and into my fletchings. I was born. Surrounded by my sleeping brothers inside the quiver, I was blind to the world outside. His spell-weaving complete, my master's hand plucked me free of my leather cocoon and bathed me in light.

I arrived in a world awash with battle and blood. My first sights, sounds, and smells were of war and all its terrors. Splintered shields and tattered bodies littered the grove of apple trees where my master fought. Not far from his feet, a War Herald lay face down, pinned to the ground by a broken spear. A tilted crown with a sword passing through it adorned his banner. Its vibrant red and white were dulled by mud ground into it by many feet. My feathers shared the colors.

A taut, waxed string slipped into the crevice of my nock. I rested lightly atop my master's gloved hand. To the left, I could see what remained of the line of archers; no more than a dozen were left standing. Even as I watched, another fell to a well-aimed spear.

"Ready!" my master commanded.

My shaft scraped against the creaking wood of the bow as I was drawn back. Directly ahead, a marauder charged in, holding an immense battle-ax high above his red-painted head. Its honed edge, already soaked with the lifeblood of our comrades, glinted in the sun.

"Aim!"

My master's hand did not waiver. He looked past the charging threat and fixed my tip on a figure standing behind a line of soldiers with tower shields, partially obscured by the weeping branches of a willow, perhaps a hundred arm-span distant from where he stood.

My feathers pressed against my master's cheek as he aligned me with his intentions. The red-painted fanatic was close enough to smell, his ax in position to cleave my master. He ignored him, too focused on his target to be distracted.

"Loose!"

His fingers relaxed. My nock took the full weight of the string just as the fanatic's ax swung in. My shaft bent and flexed painfully as the bow's energy thrust me forward. My fletchings dragged against the side of the bow and I was flying freely through air that smelled of sweat and apple blossoms.

A blow mighty enough to fell a tree crashed into my master, silencing him before I had even glanced back at him. I didn't even know his name. His mission was now mine, and the only hope of avenging his passing rested within the iron of my head. Still contorting from the force of my launch, I flew onward.

The other members of my volley soared ahead like a flock of razor-beaked birds, ready and eager to carry out orders of their own. We broke free of the cover of the treeline from where we'd been launched. Scenes of carnage panned out beneath us. Dead men, still clad in their shining armor, marked where our line had broken. Horses, cut down with swords or impaled by pikes, writhed while their crown and sword banners fluttered in the wind. The crimson tides of battle had not favored my master's forces.

The lone willow tree marked the center of the field. We had to weave our way through its branches or risk loosing the force of our launch. I looked past the branches, focusing instead on the open spaces. I missed all but a single green shoot, slicing it clean through and tasting its bitter sap. One of my brothers chose the wrong path. With a loud *thunk*, his metal-tipped head buried a finger deep into a branch as thick as a man's thigh.

We emerged through the branches, still short of our target. A small man, stooped-over from the weight of time, drove a crystal-tipped staff into the ground. The crystal flashed, spawning a miniature cyclone. A tempest lashed towards our flock like a whip. Two of my brothers succumbed instantly, their shafts stripped of feathers.

The gale struck me and grabbed at my fletchings, trying to pluck me like a chicken. Whistling and howling, it mocked me as I strained to keep my line. But my master had been strong. He gifted me with his own cunning as well as determination. I slipped through the gusts, flexing and twisting instead of fighting against them.

When I emerged, my goal was within sight. Those of my volley who had survived streaked on towards our target. One veered into the ground as a feather ripped loose.

For all our speed, we were not invisible. With painfully, almost comically slow movements, the guards closed ranks to protect their leader, raising and overlapping their shields into a solid wall of wood and leather. I knew from my brother lost in the willow branch that I could not hope to pierce it. From my position at the back of the flock, I watched as the others struggled to gain altitude in the few arm-spans left before they hit the shields.

Four failed to pull up in time and wasted themselves against the impenetrable wall. But in our first stroke of good fortune, one found a space through a carelessly held shield and struck the bearer solidly in his stomach. He doubled over in pain, dropping his shield arm just enough for me to pass overtop.

With all of my might, I curled my feathers and flexed my shaft towards the sky. My head crossed over the lip of the shield, but in the last finger-span, one of my fletchings snagged against the wood, tearing it free.

The sky and ground switched places over and over as I spun unbalanced through the air. I tried to right myself, but the force was too great. Still rolling violently and growing disoriented, I searched desperately for my objective.

Less than an arm-span ahead, the last of my brothers still flew. I realized he would lead the way. I followed him in, hoping against all reason that I could still accomplish the task my slain master had assigned me.

Still spinning, and with my sight locked onto his nock, we pressed on. I could make out a silhouette ahead, covered in chainmail, sword in hand, poised to hack us into toothpicks.

My surviving brother fell under the shadow of the blade as it slashed downward, catching him mid-shaft. The force of the blow broke his spine and he folded in half. I wanted to cry out as his splintered remains splashed harmlessly against the rings of our target's armor.

Even as I raged against the loss of my comrade, a door opened. So small was the chink, I almost missed it. As his arm came down, a thin band of flesh presented itself just below his jaw line.

Through the tumbling vertigo, I arched my keen tip towards the soft strip of pink. If I could get past the hammer-forged iron of the mail, my head would cut through the sweat-slicked skin like sheer parchment. I homed in, straining against my own fibers to complete the turn.

His arm arched back up, carrying the murderous edge of his sword up towards me. The pink ribbon of his vulnerability narrowed, along with my one chance at fulfillment.

With my last reserves of strength, I willed myself towards his neck. His sword reached me, snapping the shaft just ahead of my fletchings like a twig.

But he was too late.

My tip pierced his skin, and the rusty taste of blood washed over me. Momentum drove me deeper, through a bloodway and into his windpipe. By the time I stopped, my head had erupted back into the light.

I never learned the names of my master, nor his enemy. Never knew the reasons for their conflict. But those were not contemplations for a weapon. I had a singular purpose, and I had performed it. As my foe crashed heavily to the ground, and the life bestowed upon me returned to the ether, I felt only a profound sense of contentment.

UNERRING

The History of
A Walk in the Abyss

Compiled by Paul Genesse

I met Shane Moore at Gen Con in Indianapolis in August of 2009 when he came by my book signing for *The Golden Cord*, the first novel in my *Iron Dragon* series. He was such a nice guy and we began corresponding right after the convention. A few months later, in November of 2009, Shane emailed and asked me if I'd like to write "an orc story" for the Abyss Walker anthology he was putting together. I thought about it, and of course said "yes," as writing about orcs sounded like really good fun, and when would I ever have this chance again? I did some research, read some of Shane's *Abyss Walker* core novels, and began writing "No-Tusks" in February 2010, finishing it in March 2010.

We all thought the anthology was going to come out in late 2010, and I began reading from "No-Tusks" at conventions (ConDuit and Gen Con), where it was very well received. None of us knew it would be THREE MORE YEARS before "No-Tusks" would finally be published. The publisher who originally wanted to put out the anthology went away, and over the next couple of frustrating years opportunities came and went both for Shane and myself. The economic downturn, and a new paradigm in publishing, was wreaking havoc in the book industry.

Finally, Shane and I decided enough was enough. We would do this on our own and move ahead no matter what. Fans wanted to read "No-Tusks," and I wanted it out there. Determination once again turned out to be more important than anything else.

Fortunately, Shane had just purchased New Babel Books in early 2013, and they would be the publisher. I agreed to work as the compiler, editor, and art director. I immediately recruited Patrick M. Tracy to write a "Mungo the Giant" story, as Pat is my best friend, a great writer, and he had helped me perform "No-Tusks" at the ConDuit convention, watch the video at: vimeo.com/24400613 for a big laugh and see what the salute of the Iron Spear tribe actually looks like. This video is the reason why Pat and I will never be able to hold public office.

Pat also played the role of Mungo the Bloody Haired Giant at the release party for my third Iron Dragon novel in May of 2012 at ConDuit, when he fought in a 'Death Match' against a young actor, Anthony Holland. The awesome Mason Hall had fabricated a No-Tusks mask, and Anthony wore it for the epic combat with half the packed room playing the roles of Mungo's 'Bloody Hair Tribe' and other half in the 'Poison Spear Tribe.' It was hilarious fun. Check out the poster from the party.

DEATH MATCH!

MUNGO the Giant VS. NO TUSKS the Orc

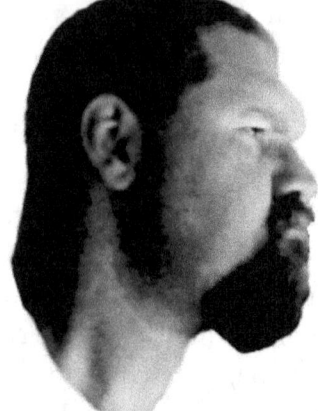

Come to the DEATH MATCH between MUNGO THE GIANT and
NO TUSKS THE ORC in the CON SUITE during the book release
Party for Book Three in the Iron Dragon Series,
The Secret Empire by Paul Genesse
Saturday Night, May 26 from 6-8 PM. Fight at 6:30!
FREE PIZZA! FREE PIZZA!
Courtesy of Paul Genesse and the Iron Spear Tribe

No-Tusks had been around for two years at this
point, and Shane and I were determined to proceed,
but other projects kept us busy, and we needed more
stories.

Shane had written a rough draft of the greyshalks
story, "A Kudekah to Remember" back in 2010 and
we ended up co-authoring that story in early 2013. We
added in Patrick S. Tomlinson's "Unerring" and an

excerpt of Tomlinson's novella, *The Wererat's Tale III*, and we had our anthology sitting at 50,000 words. Shane recruited the amazingly talented and accomplished Dan Harding to do the cover, and I tapped my good friend Zachary Hill for the interior illustrations. I had no idea that Kendall Hart had done some greyshalk sketches in 2009, and when I found out, they had to be included.

A Walk in the Abyss was finally published in May of 2013, so it could have its official release party at ConDuit, where it first opened its tusk-less mouth. There is some talk of a "No-Tusks" graphic novel, and the door is open for more stories featuring all of the main characters from these stories. The greyshalk, Petrovisk, is still young, and he has many other stories to tell. I would certainly like to know more about Mungo, and perhaps someday there will be more about devious No-Tusks and the Poison Spear Tribe.

Thank you for reading these stories, and if you enjoyed them, please tell your friends. Reviews are always appreciated and please connect with the authors on Facebook and let us know what you thought about your "Walk in the Abyss."

A toy castle is what sent fantasy author and editor Paul Genesse over the edge and into madness. Dragons and castles gave him reason to live from elementary school through college where he loved his English classes, but pursued his other passion by earning a bachelor's degree in nursing science in 1996. He is a registered nurse on a cardiac unit in Salt Lake City, Utah, where he works the night shift keeping the forces of darkness away from his patients.

Paul lives with his incredibly supportive wife, Tammy, and their collection of well-behaved frogs and moderately scary dragons. When he's not at the hospital working, or crafting novels in his basement, Paul enjoys speaking at schools to kids about writing. He's also worked as a computer game consultant, a copyeditor, and as a proofreader for a small press publisher.

He is the author of several short stories featured in *Fellowship Fantastic, The Dimension Next Door, Furry Fantastic, Imaginary Friends, Catopolis, Terribly Twisted Tales, Pirates of the Blue Kingdoms, The Pirate Witch, Steampunk'd* and more. He is also the editor of the five volumes of the demon-themed *Crimson Pact* anthology series, which you can learn more about at thecrimsonpact.com.

His first book, *The Golden Cord, Book One of the Iron Dragon* series released in 2008 as a hardcover and has become the bestselling fantasy novel Five Star Books has ever had. *The Golden Cord*, and book two, *The Dragon Hunters*, and book three, *The Secret Empire* are out now as trade paperback and eBooks; book four, *The Crystal Eye*; and the finale, book five, *The Iron Brotherhood*, are coming soon.

Learn more about the *Iron Dragon* series, check out some awesome maps, listen to podcasts, see original art, and watch videos, visit paulgenesse.com. For the latest news visit his blog, paulgenesse.blogspot.com, or friend him on Facebook.

The Golden Cord: Book One of the Iron Dragon Series:
A hunter must leave behind the woman he loves, give up all hope of survival, as he is forced to guide his most hated enemies on a suicidal journey to the lair of the dragon king.

"This is a story that's worth your time. It's almost like going back to that first fantasy novel that totally captivated you and you read it over and over again. HIGHLY RECOMMENDED."

—Russell Davis, author, editor, and President of the Science Fiction and Fantasy Writers of America

"A good mix of action, angst, and romance. The Golden Cord has fine action sequences, like many a fantasy novel, but Paul Genesse takes the time to make the protagonist and his companions much more than hack and slashers. They have hopes, fears, doubts, secret motivations, and backstories that give the action gravitas. Plenty of swordplay and slaying for the action junkies, but also plenty of self-doubt and romance for those looking for a deeper story."

—Donald J. Bingle, author of Forced Conversion

"Paul Genesse's tale is elegantly written and filled with rich, believable heroes and villains. He transports you to a vibrant fantasy world that feels so real and complex you won't want to leave. It is irresistible."

—Jean Rabe, author of the Finest Trilogy from Tor Books

Shane Moore started his writing career in 2004 after being stabbed in the line of duty as a police officer. Two years later in 2006, he received his first publishing contract. By January of 2008 he was doing so well, he retired from law enforcement and started writing full time. His dark fantasy work recently landed him with an expansion deal with Gary Gygax's former company—Troll Lord Games—for a nine-book table top role-playing game due out in 2013 and beyond.

In June of 2012 Shane launched *The Apocalypse of Enoch*, his highly anticipated end-of-days thriller that mixes elements of Alfred Hitchcock movies with *The Exorcist*. With characters like Matt Hill (Ninja Turtles), Terry Naughton (Disney), and Peter Mayhew (Star Wars) written into the story as their literal selves, *The Apocalypse of Enoch* shot to his publisher's number one bestseller. After a whirlwind tour and media blitz landing him in several TV interviews—including Saint Louis' FOX 2 with April Simpson and Tim Ezell, Shane has secured permission from the Department of the Navy for the sequel, *The Scourge of Enoch*. Shane recently signed a deal with Kissell Studios (*A-Team/Army of Two* for IDW) to adapt *The Apocalypse of Enoch* into a graphic novel.

Read the first book in the Abyss Walker core novel series.

The Abyss Walker is coming, a man who will make both gods and devils tremble.

While an obsessed king struggles to find his role in the prophecy, a young man named Lance sets out to learn more of his past. What begins as a simple task soon turns deadly as his nation continues toward war.

As tensions rise and talks waiver, one man holds the key to peace, but will they hear his plea?

"Moore's remarkable *Abyss Walker* novels have developed a devoted following, and for good reason— his immersive storytelling and the unbridled creativity make for a winning series of page-turners."

—James Kerwin, Writer/Director

"The book moves quickly, and proves a light read with an action-packed plot. Shane Moore enjoys exploring the language as he depicts scenes with great diligence. For the reader who enjoys epic fantasy movies, this is a good choice, as the book evokes a cinematic feel in pacing and scenes, from the foolish thief who runs across dinner tables to evade capture, to the evil King of Nalir who enjoys torturing his lackeys with smarmy self-satisfaction, to a dragon sprawled across his ancient treasure."

—Shroud Magazine's Book Review

The Apocalypse of Enoch by Shane Moore

Alfred Hitchcock meets The Exorcist in this end-of-days thriller!

Nations rise against nations, there are wars and rumors of wars, fires, earthquakes, floods, and droughts. Incurable disease sweep across the lands and brothers take up against their fathers. Once great nations see their economies falter, and their people scream for securities at the sacrifice of their freedoms. The answer to the world's plight will come as a thief in the night. The answer comes swiftly. The answer is . . . *The Apocalypse of Enoch*. "I will smash the door posts, and leave the doors flat down, and will let the dead go up to eat the living! And the dead will outnumber the living!" –Epic of Gilgamesh Tablet Six

"This book is a must read!!!! Well written and a very good storyline. Lots of good characters with just the right amount of creepiness. BUY IT, READ IT, tell your friends about IT!"
—Terry Naughton, Professional Illustrator/ Disney Artist

"All I have to say about 'The Apocalypse of Enoch' is this: It's Awesome!!! I'm in it . . . need I say more?"
–April Simpson, Channel 2 News in St. Louis

White Wraith by Shane Moore chronicles the story of Blaric, a young albino minotaur.

Living proof of his mother's infidelity and cursed with white fur at birth, young Blarik struggles to survive in a family that despises him. Believing that Blarik is a curse on his family by the gods, his father and mother plot to murder him and restore the family's good name. Just wanting to be loved, the poor boy endures horrific abuse in his desire to be a good son. With the sacrificial day looming, Blarik is sent away by his grandfather. Armed with nothing more than his desire to be loved by his parents and the support of a human girl from the distant village, he sets off on a wild adventure. The young bull learns many things, including what love really is. Will he and Swila perish amidst the dozens of dangers that surround his island, or will he finally reach adulthood and become the powerful champion that his grandfather believes possible?

Unsubstantiated rumors indicate that Patrick Tracy is part Sasquatch. While we have no evidence to prove or disprove this, we have been able learn some things. Patrick works as a Network Support Administrator for the Salt Lake City Corporation. He's been known to ask questions such as, "have you tried restarting it?" from time to time. Given his possibly proto-human ancestry, he is remarkably adroit with computers and technological devices. An unorthodox technician, he employs the "punch it in the face" method of computer repair.

When in his natural surroundings, he enjoys playing bass guitar, bending nails with his bare hands, and juggling cinderblocks. He also has a fondness for archery. He owns a parakeet named after the singer in a Finnish heavy metal band. People close to Patrick believe that he may be at least partially immune to cold.

Patrick has portrayed the character of Mungo in front of an audience on at least two occasions. In so doing, he has ensured that he will never be able to seek public office. When asked if this causes him any remorse, he tends to grunt softly to himself and look off to the far horizon.

Patrick writes fiction and poetry, and has been published several times in both disciplines. One of the co-creators of The Crimson Pact series, he has appeared in the four volumes that have thus far been published, most recently with his novella, Darkness of the Sun, in Volume Four. Further information about Patrick can be found at pmtracy.com.

Patrick M. Tracy's novella, "The Darkness of the Sun" is the cover story for The Crimson Pact Volume 4.

By a bullet or a blade, the Pact will have justice. A gunslinger rides down a dark road in an alternate history Old West . . . A lone woman tries to save a distant planet from a diabolical invasion . . . A rogue demon seeks vengeance on his former queen . . . Read the supernatural Western, "Darkness of the Sun," a novella by Patrick M. Tracy, and sixteen other action-packed and terrifying stories that run the gamut of urban fantasy, horror, science fiction and fantasy, with stories by Michaele Jordan, Usman T. Malik, Brett Peterson, Sarah Hans, Daniel Myers, Kelly Swails, Sarah Kanning, Valerie Dircks, John Perkins, Elizabeth Shack, Leigh Dragoon, Donald Darling, Steven Diamond, and Suzzanne Myers.

Make your mark in blood and join the Crimson Pact!

Dan was born and raised in central New Jersey where he grew up with a passion for anything to do with horror. Early on reading old horror zines, comics and books as well as an unhealthy amount of watching television. This sparked his interest in art, wanting to create his own monsters. He spent his teenage years doing art for friends and bands until he moved to PA for quite a few years where art had taken a back seat to life. In the late 90's he began to feel the urge to get back into art so he started to pick up oil painting.

Never having any formal training it was a long process but he loved every minute of it. He eventually began to get jobs doing CCG art and magazine and book covers here in the US as well as Europe and Canada. He eventually moved back to NJ where he still resides continuing to paint and work in fine art restoration.

However, Dan has never been content with his work. "I feel like I was always so suppressed by creating what publishers and game companies wanted to see that I began to get stale with art. I never really painted something I thought was cool. The past couple of years I have begun to paint what is inside me and I am excited about where my work is heading!"

"Souless" by Dan Harding

Artist and author, Zachary Hill has drawn pictures and written stories for as long as he can remember. In high school he filled up notebooks with stories and illustrations. In army basic training—after lights out—he wrote using a flashlight. During his two deployments to Iraq he wrote stories during his down time. He was always thinking about a creative project he wanted to work on, or about something he wanted to learn. He pursued his studies and graduated from Southern Virginia University with degrees in History and Art. He taught English in Italy and fell in love with the majesty of Rome and the elegant decay of Venice. He's written several books, including, *Gorgon, Uprising Italia* (a zombie apocalypse novel set in Italy) and has also been published in *The Crimson Pact Volume 5*. He illustrated *New York Times'* bestselling author Larry

Correia's *Grimnoir Chronicles* from Baen books. He loves pizza and Mountain Dew. You can find him at his fiction and art blog, Broken World, or his history blog, Minimum Wage Historian.

Grawlin, Father of Petrovisk by Zacharay Hill

Born in a haunted city in Illinois alongside the mightiest river in America, artist Kendall R. Hart was raised by 1980s pop culture and two hard-working caring human parents.

It was his frustrating inability to get Japanese toys of his beloved Godzilla that required the young sculptor to begin turning his dinosaur toys into the movie monsters he wanted. Multiple Brontosaurus (I know it was the 80s) and Pteradon toys were Frankensteined into King Gidorah, a Stegosaurus and Tyrannosaurus toys became Godzilla . . . and so a chubby kid played god through art.

Over the years Mr. Hart would hone his artistic skills in illustration, graphic design and sculpture while claiming his BFA and warning others of the perils of seeking a professional education in the visual or performing arts. (Own rental properties instead.)

Mr. Hart would discover his exact name was usurped by a character from daytime television and so summoned his middle initial into his professional name, thus becoming Kendall R. Hart.

His art and design can be found in graphic novels, non-graphic novels that depict graphic things, websites, toy and horror film concept art, America's major haunt attractions and natural history museums in the Midwest.

Currently a freelance graphic designer and life-size sculptor of monsters for the haunt and entertainment industries. He now lives in haunted city in Missouri.

His online lair is grimstonestudios.com

Petrovisk as an older greyshalk by Kendall R. Hart

Patrick S. Tomlinson is the offspring of an ex-hippie psychologist and an ex-cowboy electrician. A lifelong sci-fi fan, he discovered quite by accident that the best stories were not to be found on the silver screen, but on the gleaming white pages of books. An eclectic group of bards from Herbert to Prachett propelled him into dozens of new worlds during his formative years when he was especially vulnerable to such dubious influences.

Patrick lives in Milwaukee among a bevy of houseplants in varying stages of health, where the winters offer a wonderful opportunity to disappear into his writing cave for five months at a stretch, emerging only briefly each week to watch the Packer game. Time not spent writing is split between practicing stand-up comedy around town, training for half-marathons, undoing all the training on brewery tours, and coddling his Ford Mustang and Triumph motorcycle.

His work has appeared in *Andromeda Spaceways Inflight Magazine*, *The Crimson Pact Anthology* series, *The SFWA Bulletin*, and the *BattleCorps* website. His first book, *The Wererat's Tale: The Collar of Perdition*, was recently released by New Babel Books. Find him on Facebook on his author page.

The Wererat's Tale:
The Collar of Perdition

Excerpt from An Abyss Walker Novella
by Patrick S. Tomlinson

Chapter 1: Rat on the Run

The forest stunk of fear. Kellacun knew some of the dread was her own. Wounded and on the run from the Duke's men, her stamina was being tested like never before. She was utterly alone now, save for Kaplan, her casen tiger mount.

Strange, Kellacun mused, that a rat's only companion should turn out to be a giant feline. She let the irony play through her mind for a moment before a snapped twig and a muffled curse returned her to the here-and-now.

"Watch it," someone whispered, "Dolan said the bitch can hear a flea fart from a hundred paces."

"Must be hard to sleep, then; that filthy rat's probably covered in them."

That's going to cost you, Kellacun thought, as a vicious smirk curled the corner of her mouth. The guard was right about one thing; even in her human form, Kellacun's senses bordered on the supernatural. Maybe even crossed over, she still didn't really understand how any of it worked. The elves certainly didn't think there was much natural about wererats, and if anyone should know, it was those tree-huggers.

She took a long, slow pull of air into her nose. There were three of them. Smells of sweat with a trace of perfume and floral notes mingled with the dirt and moss of the forest. The exotic flower smell was from a caladais, a favorite flower of one of the Duke's courtesans. The palace was filled with them at this time of year.

Kellacun grimaced. That meant these three weren't just the flunky tax-collectors and poachers she'd bested with such ease. They were drawn from the reserve of the Duke's personal guard. They would be better trained, better equipped, and the most blindly loyal. It also explained why they had continued pursuing through the night after the rest of the guards had fallen behind.

But their cushy position inside the palace had its drawbacks. The men were totally out of their element, unsupported in a dense forest in the dead of night. Their eyes would not be accustomed to such near darkness. At least they were smart enough not to carry torches.

Kellacun searched the forest floor for Kaplan, but the immense tiger's fur proved to be too good of camouflage even for her. Even though she couldn't see Kaplan, she knew what her mount was doing, maneuvering silently to find the best ambush position, then waiting to strike. She'd seen house cats play the same game with mice and ground squirrels in the alleys of Central City for years. Kaplan was no different from them, except for the extra ton of muscle, teeth, and claws.

Kellacun stood to her full height, but winced as a fresh jolt of pain shot up through her leg. She leaned back against the tree trunk and swallowed a scream.

Her leg had been broken, shattered really, in a fight with a Nonul only two days before. And even though her accelerated healing had knit the bone, her nerves still protested loudly whenever she tried to put her full weight on it.

The rest of her body wasn't fairing much better. Her swordfight with Grascon had left deep cuts and stab wounds to her back and legs, and the enchanted blade meant they would heal normally. Her demon-skin armor had already mended, however, which was fortunate. It felt as though the snug armor was the only thing holding her shredded body together.

She wasn't in any condition to fight three trained killers, but her aching bones begged for rest. She needed to stop running, to sleep, and to heal. Her odds of survival shrank with every extra hour of exhaustion that piled on. Kellacun decided to take her chances and make a stand. She could count on surprise to fell her first victim, but then she'd be flanked by the two survivors. Hopefully, Kaplan would know a good opportunity when she saw it.

Kellacun decided to ramp up the men's fear by changing to her feral form. The sacrifice in finesse would be more than offset by the extra strength it afforded her, not to mention the terror it would bring out in her quarry. Panting softly, she willed her inner rat forward. The change was . . . disconcerting. Her skin prickled like it was swarming with ants as thick black fur burst forth. Her elongating jaw dislocated until her nose caught up. She reset it with a click of her now chisel-like teeth. Her fingernails felt like they were being pulled out with pliers as they grew into thick, black claws. It took real effort not to scream.

Her armor stretched and morphed to fit her changing shape. A few seconds later and the painful transformation was at an end. Kellacun slowly drew the thin, enchanted blade she'd won off the first assassin the Duke had sent for her life. Her father's sabre would remain in its sheath; she wasn't sure she had the strength to wield it.

The lush forest canopy blocked nearly all moonlight from reaching the floor, so Kellacun didn't need to worry about her sword glinting and betraying her presence. Her prey was close enough now that her wild-form eyes could size up the guards individually. The man at point was the smallest, but also had the most baubles on his jerkin. The two larger men trailed behind him like loyal dogs. That answered who to take down first.

Their leader identified, Kellacun maneuvered, quiet as a temple mouse. A small, yet noisy corner of her mind still railed against the violence she was about to commit. Only a few short months ago, she had been a simple mason's daughter, blessed with loving parents and the affections of the Duke's son. That all changed late one night; the night her parents were murdered, her lover abandoned her, and the animal lurking deep inside came bursting out. It had been an incessant fight for survival and vengeance every moment since. The next few minutes would be no different.

The short man at the head of the line felt his way through the forest, one hand held out to sweep branches from his face, the other on the hilt of his sabre. Kellacun ducked behind a tree a few paces ahead of him, then pulled back a branch and held it tight. Relying on her black fur to keep her hidden, she waited until the man was only a step away, then let the branch go.

With a sharp crack, the spiny branch snapped the lead guard right in the face. He shouted out in surprise and pain. His left hand grabbed his face involuntarily, while the right fumbled to draw his sabre. He didn't get the chance. Kellacun ran out from her hiding place and grabbed the guard's wrist with her free hand, then plunged her teeth into his exposed throat. The sickening taste of hot, rusty blood exploded into her mouth. His screaming stopped abruptly as he collapsed into the leaves.

To their credit, the other two men didn't panic or run. Instead, their sabers sang pure notes as they were pulled free of their scabbards. Yet their blades cut through empty air, searching in vain for the indistinct target. One slash did manage to hit home . . . into one of the guard's thighs.

"Idiot! You cut me!"

"Where's Tylus?"

Kellacun's raspy, rodent voice echoed through the woods. "He's bleeding out on the ground. Leave now unless you wish to join him."

"Not likely," shouted one of the guards, "on either count." They stopped swinging pointlessly, then formed up back-to-back, sabre tips out.

Kellacun answered with a dashing attack, slashing at the wounded guard's leg, but her blade's accuracy suffered greatly from her injured back muscles. She managed only a glancing blow, shrugged off by his leather armor. His answering slash was far more effective, despite his near blindness. The sharp bite of his sword cut deeply into the gap between her chest and waist armor, but it lacked the burning Kellacun had come to associate with enchanted weapons. The wound started to heal immediately.

Buoyed with the knowledge the guards' weapons could not hurt her . . . much, Kellacun pressed the attack. With her light rapier, she thrust, quickly and repeatedly, trying to tire her pursuers as they defended themselves with heavier sabers. It was the same tactic Grascon had used against her only hours before, except they were nowhere near his level of swordsmanship. Neither was she, however. Her muscles burned from the effort of working around so many injuries. She knew the fight needed to be over, quickly and decisively, or her tale would end there and then.

Kellacun's ears twitched as she heard a rustling sound charging up behind her. She ducked. As if Kaplan had been listening to her thoughts, the enormous black cat dove over Kellacun's crouching body and crashed into one of the guards. Her immense weight took the man completely off his feet. Kaplan pinned him to the ground and closed her jaws around his neck and face, suffocating him.

Outnumbered by monsters, the survivor decided to drop his sword and take his chances.

"Oh, I see you can count, at least," Kellacun taunted.

"You have me, no need to rub dirt in it." His back

was straight and voice tremble free. Whatever terror he felt, the guard was controlling it very well.

"What's your name?"

"Yvoni Fellax."

"Yvoni Fellax?" she repeated menacingly.

"Miss."

"That's better. A gentleman of your station must remember his manners, otherwise you'd be no better than—"

"A rat."

Kellacun lashed out with her claws, raking them across his shoulder blades. He winced, but made no sound.

"Fellax is a name of the provinces, why answer to the Duke in Central City?"

"Conscripted, Miss, along with my brother, who you killed in this forest not three days ago."

Kellacun studied him for a moment, then sighed. "I have no quarrel with clan Fellax, Yvoni. You and your kin were in my way, nothing more. But here's the news, your Duke must not hold you in very high esteem, sending you out against such a dangerous opponent with weapons he knew full well couldn't do much more than irritate me."

His face twisted in confusion. "What of it?"

"I have no desire to battle with clan Fellax more than I have already. My only grief is with the Duke. He was willing to throw your life away; you have no more reason to trust him than I."

Yvoni listened intently, not that he had much choice. "And you have a proposal, I assume?"

"Yes, as a matter of fact." Kellacun reached for the dagger at the young man's side and drew it. He braced for an attack, but none came. Instead, she inspected the blade; fine craftsmanship, keen, but not enchanted. It wasn't even silver. She shook her head at Dolan's callous disregard for his own people. Then, she steeled herself and grabbed one of her thin, furry ears.

With a quick slash, Kellacun cut the ear free of her head. The pain was intense, but even more disorienting was the effect it had on her hearing. The sounds of the forest seemed to come at her from two different distances. She hoped her guess that it would grow back was right.

Apparently, Yvoni could see a little better than he'd been leading on. He jumped back in shock. "Why the hell did you do that?"

Kellacun stuffed the severed ear into the man's waistband. "So that you can go home and tell the Duke I'm dead. I have another matter to attend to, which would be easier without his assassins constantly on my tail."

Yivoni looked unconvinced, so she tried to sweeten the pot. "Think about it, Fellax, you'll be greeted as a hero. I know there's a healthy reward on my hide, enough to spend the rest of the year drunk and atop the wench of your choice."

"Everyone knows you've sworn to kill the Duke at any price. What happens to me when you come back? He'll know I lied about killing you and I'll be executed."

Kellacun pulled her lips back, revealing teeth still stained with the blood of the first guard. "Then you'll need to help me kill him before he figures it out."

Yvoni's spine stiffened to parade-ground readiness. "And if I refuse to go along with this deception and coup?"

Kellacun looked over her shoulder to where Kaplan was unabashedly gorging herself on her prey's liver. "I wasn't offering you a choice."

"I see." Yvoni weighed his non-options for a heartbeat, then looked Kellacun right in her bulging black eyes. "Looks like you have a partner."

"Excellent. Now, I must be going. I have business to the South." She turned and walked into the night, letting her human form reassert itself. Kaplan swallowed a last gulp, then trotted off after her.

"Wait! How am I supposed to get back?"

Kellacun chuckled. "You found your way in, Fellax. You can find your way back out."

Joshua paced through his room, slowly eroding a valley into the marble floor. His breakfast of poached syliban eggs and fresh cut tokur fruit sat untouched on the oak table. His eyelids pulled down heavily, but he couldn't sleep. So he paced, like a wild animal surveying the boundaries of its cage.

The door creaked open. He'd have to remind the servants to grease the hinges. His father, Duke Dolan, stepped through.

"I'm told you haven't eaten, Joshua."

Joshua glanced at the plate of cold food and

smirked. "Your spies penetrate even my bed chambers, Father?"

"Of course. If only my agents were so efficient in the rest of the city. What vexes you? Still troubled by that rat girl?"

Joshua's head dipped. "I must be transparent as glass."

"Only because I know you so well, my son. What is not clear to me is the target of your frustration."

Joshua felt himself treading on thin ice indeed. His next words needed to be carefully chosen. "Kellacun, father," he paused, "and myself, I suppose."

Dolan took a seat at the table and nibbled on a piece of fruit. "You, how so?"

"Because, I was in love with her. I was preparing to ask your permission to marry her. I never suspected her true nature. How could my judgment have been so blind?"

Dolan just chuckled. "You suffer the same affliction as all healthy young men, my boy. Nothing kills a man's reason faster than fluttering eyelashes and rosy lips. The weapons women wield are softer than our own, but just as deadly. Never forget that."

Joshua nodded. "I won't." He walked over to the ceremonial arsenal hanging on his wall. He made a show of perusing the selection of blades, maces, and shields before pulling a thin silver dagger from its sheath. "In fact, I'd like to turn that very weapon on its owner."

Dolan's eyebrow twitched. "What are you proposing?"

"Think, father. Every assassin you've sent after Kellacun has returned in a box, or several. That thieving rat Pavco and his pathetic 'guild' have failed as well, possibly by design."

"And you believe you can succeed where they have failed?"

"Yes, absolutely."

Dolan shook his head. "I'm afraid not, Joshua, I won't risk my only heir. That bitch hasn't just killed my best men, she's slaughtered them like cattle. You've grown into a fine swordsman, but you don't have the experience of your masters. One of whom fell to Kellacun's blades, I would remind you."

"But that's the beauty of it, father. I won't have to fight her. She wants you dead, not me. You saw it with your own eyes last night. She wouldn't fight me, even as I tried to plunge my blade into her heart."

"And then you promised to kill her. An oath she is unlikely to forget, Joshua."

"I'll say it was out of anger, in the panic to protect you."

Dolan's face became solemn as he weighed the proposal.

"I can do this, Father. Let me prove my worth with this errand."

"Do you really believe you have the fortitude to kill your first love?"

"You misjudge me. My family and this castle are my first love. The lust I once felt for Kellacun pales in comparison."

The Duke smiled. "Well played, my boy. Very well,

you have my permission to undertake this mission. Indeed, it will be your first official assignment."

"I will not fail, Father."

"I'm sure of it, Joshua. But be wary. Central City will need a new Duke one day, and I don't want to start another one from scratch."

kellakun

Chapter 2: River Rats

Days in the forest started to merge together. The thick canopy of leaves and intertwining branches kept the ground in a near perpetual dusk as it was, making it difficult for Kellacun to get a sense of the time. Night fell with alarming suddenness, and carried its own dangers. A bear had taken a strong interest in her on the second night, or more specifically, the meat on her bones. But a brief stare-down and some growling with Kaplan convinced him it wouldn't be worth the fight.

They had been walking through the forest for almost a week. Kellacun could scarcely believe how far it extended. Trails interrupted here and there, and the occasional clearing gave her just enough sky to confirm that they were still headed south. Despite proving to be a much better hunter of men than game, Kellacun ate well. Kaplan's skills more than made up for her shortcomings, and she was surprisingly eager to share her kills. Kellacun couldn't help but feel a bit like the tiger was treating her like an oddly-shaped cub.

Still, the forest's size and density were its greatest assets for Kellacun at the moment, despite the slow going. Her new friend Fellax should have reached Central City by now and reported her "death" to Duke

Dolan, provided he hadn't met a bear of his own. It was her job now to keep from creating any rumors of her escape until they were well beyond the reach of the duke's spies and contacts. The further she traveled undetected, the safer she would be.

She realized that her hand had absently started rubbing at her missing ear. A bud of a new lobe had started to grow in, but it was still small and itched terribly. Apparently replacing whole body parts was a steeper hill to climb than just repairing damaged ones, even for her enhanced healing powers. Fortunately, Kaplan's were the only eyes around to see her disfigurement.

Kellacun struggled yet again to keep despair at bay. Her wild form aside, she was not a creature of the outdoors. Until a few short months ago, her entire life had passed by ensconced in the protective, if dirty, confines of Central City's barrier walls. The forest's sounds and odors were as alien to her as she had been to the elves. But as little as she knew about the forest, she knew less still about where she was headed.

The Kingdom of Nalir lay so far to the south that Kellacun had only met a handful of traders that hailed from it. They were a rough-and-tumble bunch, but she supposed a month's travel over river and road had more than a little to do with their temperaments by the time they reached Central City's gates. Of their King, Hector, she knew nothing at all, except that Grascon believed she could find work with him. Any King that would employ a foreign wererat assassin was probably a shady enough character to be wary of in the first place. She chuckled at the thought.

Kaplan's ears perked up suddenly. She let out a low, challenging grumble a moment before Kellacun's good ear picked up the intruder. Her enchanted rapier was drawn in a flash as she spun to face the unannounced newcomer. As quickly as she'd brought the tip to bear, she dropped it again.

"What do *you* want?" The question came out in a heavy sigh.

"Good to see you again as well, wererat," replied the centaur.

"Caballus, wasn't it?"

The horseman nodded.

"You made it plain when we met how you felt about my . . . people."

Arms as thick as Kellacun's thighs crossed over Caballus's chest. "That was before you fought against those sewer rats from the city, defending my elf friends in the cave."

Kellacun snorted as she sheathed her rapier. "Fat lot of good my help did them, considering I was the only survivor."

"Still, you tried, which is more than I can say for some of us in the woods."

He sounded troubled, almost wistful. Not something Kellacun would have expected from a fey. "You wanted to stand with the elves?"

He nodded.

"Well then why didn't you?"

His smile conveyed anything but happiness. "Fey are not nearly as independent as you might think.

There are traditions to follow."

"You know what my father used to say about traditions?"

Caballus shook his head.

"Traditions are what we call things when nobody can remember why we keep doing them."

Caballus craned his head back and let out a belly laugh that shook the trees to their roots. "Your father is a clever one, I think."

A fresh pang of guilt and anger shot through Kellacun's stomach. "Yes, he was."

The centaur's mood dimmed in response to her pain. He looked for a moment as though he would offer comfort, but thought better of it. "At any rate, I felt compelled to repay the blood you shed for my friends, even if the gesture is only a token." He reached a big, calloused hand into a knapsack strapped to his horse-body. It reemerged holding a familiar-looking shape swathed in linen.

He slowly unwrapped the cloth, revealing her missing trophy. "I believe you dropped this."

Kellacun surged forward, gently taking the offered blade from Caballus's hands. "How did you get this? Quasias still had it with him when, ah . . . "

"When something turned him into foie gras?" Caballus smirked. "Yes, I'd be interested to know how you did that."

"I'm afraid there won't be a repeat of that performance."

"Pity, the forest has some pests that could use clearing out. Listen, you've earned that blade twice now; once when you took it from the Al-Kalidian, and again when you killed the birdman. Try to keep a better hold of it, though."

Kellacun slid the thin rapier into its waiting sheath. "Thank you."

"None needed. Our debts cancel now, Wererat. You're nearing the forest's edge. By the end of the day, you'll reach the river. If you hurry, you can catch a ride with a bargeman named Steyer. He can take you south much faster."

"Thanks, but I doubt anyone's going to give passage to a girl and her giant tiger."

"Steyer won't mind, he's blind."

Kellacun snorted. "Blind, maybe, but surely he can still hear and smell."

Caballus winked conspiratorially. "Plausible deniability."

"Ah, I see . . . Caballus?"

The centaur raised an eyebrow, prodding her to continue.

"There will always be someone to carry on tradition. If there's something you believe is worth fighting for, maybe you should be the one fighting."

The horseman stamped a hoof nervously, unsure of what to say.

"Surely you're not afraid?" Kellacun asked incredulously. "Look at you, you could be your own cavalry charge!"

Caballus stroked his short beard thoughtfully. "Hmm, I suppose I could at that. Hardly seems fair, does it?"

"Fighting seldom is. Good day, my … acquaintance."

The horseman smiled thinly, then cupped a hand beside his mouth to whisper. "You may call me friend, Kellacun. Just not too loudly."

"Understood. Be well."

The centaur gave a small bow, then turned back into the forest and disappeared as suddenly as he'd came. Kellacun rubbed the pommel of her reclaimed sword, scratched Kaplan behind the ear, then continued south.

The fey's advice proved useful. Kellacun pressed on through the thinning forest, emerging on the banks of the Dawson River just in time to catch Steyer casting off his lines. She somehow managed to convince Kaplan to remain concealed in the bushes, despite the language barrier between them. The cat was proving to be very cunning. Kellacun wasn't sure if she should feel relieved or concerned.

She waved a hand at the bargeman to get his attention, then slapped herself on the forehead when she remembered the man was blind.

"Hail Steyer!" she called out.

On the deck of his barge, the man turned an ear towards the unfamiliar voice. "Who calls for me?" he shouted in reply.

Kellacun walked down the sandy bank towards the barge. It seemed to be little more than a couple dozen empty whiskey barrels lashed to planks that formed the deck. Still, it appeared solid enough for her purposes.

"I was sent by Caballus, he said you're known to take on passengers."

"I am. What's your name, young lady?"

"He also said you weren't one to ask too many questions," she said as sweetly as possible.

"Ah, I see. One of those stories. Well lass, in that case I have only two questions; how much weight, and how do you plan to pay?"

The tension left Kellacun's shoulders. "It's just me and my, um, horse. So call it eighty stone. And I have silver."

Steyer held out a wrinkled hand shaped by decades spent pulling rope. Kellacun dropped a pair of coins into his palm. He held them up to his ear and clinked them together, then touched them to his tongue. "Fine, fine. How far are you going?"

"Nalir."

"End of the line, huh? I'll need two more of these." He rubbed the coins together.

"And you shall have them when we reach Nalir."

His eyes continued staring over her shoulder, but creases appeared on his forehead. "Trying to dupe poor blind Steyer, are you girl?"

"No, sir," Kellacun shook her head, "my coin purse grows light is all. I must be sure I get what I pay for."

Steyer's weatherworn face softened. "Okay, lass, hold onto your money. I don't mind earning my keep. Better bring your horse aboard, I'm ready to sail."

"Thank you." Kellacun turned and waved a hand to her mount in the bushes. Once again interpreting her intentions correctly, Kaplan stood and slinked towards the river bank. Kellacun wasn't sure how the giant cat was going to feel about being in the middle of so much water.

Steyer cast off the last of his lines, then bent over to grab a pair of long, thick boards. Years moving cargo had given him a strong back, and he hefted both of them with ease. "Give me a hand with these."

"Where do they go?"

"They're ramps, girl, for your—" Steyer was interrupted by the sudden impact of Kaplan's immense weight landing on the far side of the deck. Steyer and Kellacun fought to stay afoot under the pitching barge, "—horse?"

"Sorry," Kellacun purred, "she fancies herself a jumper."

"Uh-huh. Funny shoes you have on her, too. Most hooves go, 'clop-clop.'"

"Well . . . "

Steyer put up a hand. "I don't care, miss. Just keep whatever it is from eating me and we can stay friends, okay?"

"Okay," Kellacun replied somewhat sheepishly.

"Get your 'horse' to stay in the middle of the barge, and don't let it move around too much." Steyer stuck a pole into the muddy bank and pushed off. "And keep it away from my lamb jerky!"

The barge sailed south through the night. With her eyes fully adjusted to the sliver of light from the moon, Kellacun stood on the prow and watched the land drift by. Every moment that passed took her further away from what had once been her home than she had ever traveled. But further from what? Further from the bodies of her parents? Further from Joshua and their dead love? Further from the den of thieves and assassins paid to slaughter her?

Maybe further was better after all, she decided. The river was quiet, with only the shuffling sound of Steyer's sandals as he moved down the length of the barge with his pole. There was little traffic on the Dawson at this hour. Most every boat, barge, and canoe had pulled ashore until morning returned. Of course, the dark provided little challenge for a blind pilot.

"You are still awake, Miss?"

"Yes, I'm a bit of a night owl."

"I'm not, I've been trolling this creek since before you were born. Still struggle to keep awake some nights."

Kellacun's forehead rumpled with questions. She picked one at random to start with. "How do you know how old I am?"

"What? A blind man can't hear the silky sound of a youthful voice? Or the smell of a girl just coming into womanhood? Or the . . . " He breathed in through his nose, carefully sampling confusing odors. "Or a horse that smells suspiciously like a pile of wet barn cats."

"Um . . . "

"I said I didn't care."

"Thank you."

"It's better for both of us."

"Okay, but why not just work during the day?"

Steyer snorted a laugh. "Ironically, because there were too many 'captains' with perfectly good eyes who couldn't find the time to use them. I got tired of replacing barrels every time a distracted boat blundered into me. The worst part was I almost always had to pay for the damage to both boats. Everyone knew the accidents *must* have been the blind man's fault."

"I'm sorry. That's terrible."

"Don't worry, lass. I may grumble, but my new schedule has opened up new . . . business opportunities for me. Passengers like yourself, who prefer to move unseen."

Kellacun couldn't help but smirk. "You're perfect for the job, my friend. I'm sure you have stories to tell."

"No, I don't, which is what you paid for."

"Of course."

Steyer turned his head and listened to the frogs as they chirped the night away, ever optimistic in love.

"I have learned one thing that I can share freely."

"I'd be grateful."

"The river makes running easy. The current carries you from whatever troubles you, fast and far. Problem is, there always comes a time to stop running. And the further away the river takes you, the harder the journey home will be."

"I understand, but I'm not running. I'm here to keep a promise."

"Promises are easy to come by in Nalir, but hard to keep."

"Okay, do you have practical wisdom in addition to the folksy, sage advice?"

Steyer smirked. "I might. What do you want to know?"

"How well do you know Nalir and her King?"

"King Hector is an impressive man. Then again, one would have to be to beat Nalir's festering swamps into a functioning kingdom, even if only just. He is ambitious, cunning, and ruthless. Be wary of that one."

"I thought you said he was a good man?"

"I said he was an *impressive* man, that doesn't mean *good*. Often it means precisely the opposite. Hector is not needlessly cruel; he does not relish inflicting suffering as some tyrants do, but neither does he scrupulously avoid it. Whatever vision he holds for Nalir's future, it's his first priority. His people are tools to further that vision, nothing more."

"What of a merc called Bladewright? Do you know anything about him?"

"That old half-blood? Stay clear of him."

"Half-blood? What do you mean?"

"He's half-orc, and a dangerous one at that."

Kellacun unconsciously rested a palm on the pommel of her saber. "What makes him so dangerous?"

"Being tainted with orc blood will make anyone twitchy, but he embraced his violent heritage. He was a fearsome warrior for many years, but now he's a warrior without a war. He turned to drink to quell his demons."

"Great," Kellacun sighed, "another drunk."

"A drunk? Heavens no, lass. Drunks are sloppy amateurs. He's elevated it to an art form." Steyer pointed to the barrels that kept his barge afloat. "Personally witnessed him drain one o' these whisky barrels in one evening, then gift it to me to repair my boat."

"Well that was . . . nice of him."

"Oh aye, he can be very friendly, but his mood changes quicker than a mountain wind. And you never can tell what's going to flip the lever."

Kellacun had no more questions for him, and Steyer fell silent. The barge drifted down the river guided by only an occasional nudge of Steyer's pole against the steep banks. Kellacun wondered at how he could tell when the boat was coming too close, so she closed her eyes. She felt the boat rolling gently against the waves and ripples, listened to the trickling of the water against the barrels. Her ear still itched, but had grown back to nearly full size and no longer impeded her hearing. The calls of frogs and crickets merged into a harmony of notes until one was almost indistinguishable from the other.

The calls ebbed, then died away entirely on the nearby stretch of beach. On cue, Steyer pushed his pole against the river bed, casting the barge back into the current. So simple, yet so easy to overlook. Kellacun resolved to spend more time honing all of her new senses.

It had been a long, difficult few days. For the first time since her failed attempt on the Duke's life, she felt at relative ease. There were no dangers on the raft, and those who had been pursuing her drifted further away with each league. Content with her unexpected security, Kellacun nestled up against Kaplan's soft black fur. The tiger couldn't purr, but she let out a satisfied sigh and extended a heavy, protective paw over her friend's chest. Warmed by the cat's body heat, Kellacun sank into a deep, dreamless sleep. Kellacun felt something probing her side. Her eyes snapped open, but were blinded by a sudden flash of sunlight.

She lashed with one hand, finding an arm touching her ribs, while long, black claws grew reflexively from her other hand in preparation.

"Easy, girl. It's time to wake up. We're in Nalir."

The voice was Steyer's. She had slept straight through the rest of the night and well into the morning. Her eyes adjusted quickly to see the bargeman leaning over her, offering a hand to help her up. She accepted.

"What time is it?"

"Sorry, that's one thing I'm not brilliant at."

Kellacun chuckled softly. "I suppose not. Thank you for the lift." She reached into her purse and turned over a pair of silver coins. "The balance of my fare, as promised."

"Much obliged, Miss."

Steyer held up his hands. "I never even saw you," he said with a mischievous grin.

"Right." Kellacun gathered herself up. Kaplan yawned, and stretched out her legs in a decadent display of feline laziness. With considerable effort, she raised herself up from the deck and slunk off towards the pier.

A pair of dock workers extended a rickety boarding ramp to meet the barge. To their credit, they only paused for a heartbeat at the sight of Kaplan siting on her haunches. Obviously, stranger things than a pretty girl and her giant cat had come through Nalir. Kellacun helped Steyer tie off his mooring lines before walking down the plank herself. She turned to wave at the bargeman, then slapped herself a second time. "Smooth sailing, Steyer!"

The old sailor turned and faced the sound of her voice. "When you're ready for the long trip home, look me up. Oh, and you might find what you're looking for at the Bog Water tavern."

"Thanks!" Kellacun spun around on a heel and started down the pier.

The Dawson River had widened into a vast delta plain, rife with sandbars and mangroves. The odorous swamps of Nalir spread before her, crisscrossed with a web of timber dykes and earthen levies. Roads made of roughly hewn stone sat atop the wider, taller levies. In the distance, a hill clawed for the sky. It was the only feature on the horizon. A road spiraled its way around the hill, before reaching an enormous walled keep, perched atop the hill like a stone crown. Built up around the base was a ramshackle ring of buildings. If one was feeling generous, it could even be called a city.

Wagons carrying trade goods from the port streamed towards the city, while carts carrying mud from the swamps streamed towards the river's edge. The buildings surrounding the port seemed limited to warehouses, trader's stalls, and stables. Kellacun was confident the Bog Water wouldn't be found here. She got the attention of one of the more . . . colorful-looking dock workers. It wasn't difficult; he was already staring at her.

"Good morning," she said cheerfully. "I'm looking for—"

"Don't say a stable." The dockman pointed a gnarled finger at Kaplan. "Ain't nobody going to board *that* thing."

"I was actually going to ask about a tavern, the Bog Water? Do you know where I can find it?"

"The lady likes to live dangerously."

Kellacun stroked the black fur of Kaplan's neck. "Wouldn't you if you had pets like her?"

"Ha! I might at that, girl." He jabbed a thumb towards the ring city surrounding the hilltop castle. "It's on the far side, corner of Determination and Perseverance."

Kellacun cocked an eyebrow. "Strange names for streets."

"Hector's idea. S'posed to remind us little people of our morals."

"How's that working?"

"Hasn't taken root with me, but mum always said my head wasn't very fertile ground."

Kellacun smirked. "Thanks, I'll let you back to work." The laborer tipped his cap and returned to coiling rope. Kellacun turned to the hill, which she estimated to be several miles distant. She looked at Kaplan and toyed with the idea of taking a ride, but decided against it. Her wounds were close to healed, and the day spent languishing on Steyer's barge had left her legs and hips stiff. A brisk walk would do them good.

Chapter Three:
The Swamps of Nalir

It was Dolan's turn to pace. The floor of his throne room was clad in an intricate pattern of creamy marble and red granite, with silver trim between the joints. It had not come cheaply, and had required the labors of a dozen masons for nearly a month. Masons Dolan had executed soon thereafter when it was discovered they did not harbor the best of intentions for the Duke's continued rule.

He'd watched the day before as Joshua, his only son and heir, had saddled up the fastest horse in the Duke's stables and departed on his first assignment outside Central City's walls. An assignment, Dolan learned this morning, that may have been entirely in vain, but there was no way to tell Joshua that now.

Dolan made a note from now on only to lend operatives his *second* fastest horse.

The door creaked open and Vical, Dolan's Chief of Staff, poked his head through. "Sire, the, um, 'leader' of the Thieves Guild has arrived as you requested."

"Show him in, Vical."

"Very good, sir. Will you require refreshments?"

"Oh, I don't think we need to waste good wine on

the likes of him."

"As you wish." Vical's head withdrew. A moment later, the door swung open and disgorged the portly, disheveled form of Pavco into Dolan's presence. It was obvious that both men would be much happier once the encounter had concluded.

Dolan nodded to his guest. "Pavco."

"Your grace," the wererat thief said sarcastically. "Don't worry about the wine; I have better stock at home."

"I'm sure." Dolan motioned for his guest to have a seat in an elegantly carved high-back chair. "And more comfortable furniture, no doubt."

Pavco let his girth fall into the chair. Wooden legs creaked under the unexpected burden. "Eh, not really. The rats tend to steal all the stuffing for nesting. Difficult little buggers to eradicate." His face twisted into a proud grin. His meaning was not lost on Dolan, but he was being clever beyond his capacities. The thief was overconfident in his strength, but that was fine with the duke. Overconfident adversaries made mistakes. All a smart man need do was keep out their way and wait.

"Funny you should say that, because our rodent problem is exactly what I called you here to discuss."

"I told you already, she's gone. Deep into the forest with that tiger she found. And Grascon's disappeared too. His head is suddenly very valuable because of that little stunt."

"It continues to amaze me how much trouble an entire den of wererat thieves has killing one little wererat girl. Aren't thieves supposed to be good at finding things that are well hidden?"

"Don't question my dedication, Dolan. I lost over a dozen men to that bitch during the forest raid, 'sides, it's not like you've done much better. How many guards of yours has she scrapped? Not to mention that giant iron toy you handed her."

Dolan held up a hand. "That's enough. We can agree that Kellacun has been a most persistent thorn in both of our sides, but that may have changed. As it happens, she was found in the deep of the forest by three of my personal reserve guards."

"Really? Who found *their* bodies?"

"No one," Dolan said as he walked for the door. He opened it a crack and whispered to Vical, "Send him in."

Dolan withdrew as another man dressed in the uniform of the Duke's Reserve entered the throne room. He was medium height, powerfully built, yet walked with a pronounced limp.

"Pavco, may I introduce Yvoni Fellax, fresh from an excursion to the forest. He has an interesting story to tell us."

The fetid plains of Nalir were deceptively broad. Kellacun and Kaplan had been walking for well over an hour and seemed only marginally closer to the ring city. The levy they tread upon ran parallel to a row of windmills bigger than any she'd ever seen.

On a ridgeline outside Central City, she'd seen smaller machines capture the wind to turn mill stones and grind wheat and corn. Here in Nalir, however, they turned giant screw-tubes, sucking the swamps dry of water and spilling it over the tops of the dykes and back into the sea.

Once drained, each walled plot of land was left with a thick layer of incredibly fertile muddy soil. These were then turned to agriculture. Kellacun had seen rice, barley, beats, potatoes, lithurgal beans, even grape vines growing in the reclaimed land.

The miles rolled past into the afternoon. Every half mile or so, a set of flood gates were cut into the dyke. The gates angled inwards, propped up from beneath with thick timbers. Strangely, the timbers were cut straight through the middle, with large chains secured below the cuts. It took Kellacun several minutes to puzzle out the purpose of the strange arrangement. With a jerk of the chains, the timbers would buckle and collapse, dropping the gate and letting the ocean flood the land once more. It was only then that she noticed the road she and Kaplan walked on actually sat below the dykes.

Any army intent on invading Nalir would quickly find themselves drowned by the sea. The castle hill would effectively be turned into an island, requiring a navy to lay siege to it. The entire kingdom had been designed from the ground up to be a booby trap. Steyer had been right; King Hector was an impressive man indeed.

The city grew closer, and the smells of swamp, livestock, and agriculture began to mingle with the scents of smith shops, fermentation, tanning, and the great unwashed masses inside Kellacun's nose. Tendrils of grey and black smoke rose from a hundred different chimneys, clouding a clear view of the approach to the castle at the hill's summit.

Kellacun stepped ahead of Kaplan as they approached a check point of sorts. The ring city presented no wall, mote, or other obvious defenses. Instead, a wooden gate straddled the road's stones. A small, rickety sentry hut stood to one side, while an equally rickety sentry manned the gate.

"Halt!" called out a voice that sounded like the winds of time themselves. The ancient sentry was armed with only a short spear, which pulled double-duty as a cane.

Kellacun stopped as instructed and waited politely for the old man to shuffle around the barricade. He drew himself up to his full height, which was still a handspan shorter than Kellacun. "What brings you to Nalir, young lady?"

"Business," Kellacun replied, "of a private nature."

"How long will you be staying with us?"

"I'm not sure yet, but perhaps for a while."

"Very well, but your, ah, friend there will need to stay outside the city."

Kellacun had been afraid something like this was coming. "Are you sure that's a good idea? You have an awful lot of sheep and cattle wandering around out here."

"Better missing lambs than missing people, young Miss."

She was about to object, until remembering the

fallen guard in the forest, and the unsettling look of contentment on Kaplan's face as she dined on him. "You may have a point, there."

"We have quite a feral pig problem in the fields, there's even a bounty. Perhaps your friend can be put to good use."

Kellacun scratched the tiger behind an ear. "What do you think, Kaplan? Can you stick to pork for a few days?" The cat chuffed happily. Whether it was in understanding or just appreciation of a good scratch, Kellacun couldn't say. "All right, I'm trusting you. No two-legged meals, agreed?"

Kaplan regarded her with a pained expression, then plopped down on her haunches. With that sorted, the frail sentry swung open the timber gate, allowing Kellacun to sweep past.

"Enjoy your stay," he called to her back.

Once past the gate, the familiar sights and sounds of the city surrounded Kellacun. Unlike the crowded, chaotic streets of Central City, though, Nalir's ring was new and organized. The very oldest structures had been built less than a generation ago. The broad streets were arranged in an orderly grid of concentric circles and radiating lines. The city's youth and order did little to advance cleanliness, however. Building materials consisted mainly of fired bricks made of clay and manure, which left the city with a... uniquely earthy odor.

Evidence abound in gutters running to either side of the streets that the city lacked the network of sewer tunnels Kellacun and the Thieves Guild had come to rely on back home. But of course it would, she realized. The water level must be only a few inches below the surface. There would be nowhere for sewers to run to.

She found Determination Street two rings in, after Strength and Unity, and followed it to the right. If the dockworker's word proved reliable, Bog Water would be on the opposite side of the castle hill anyway. She studied the castle as she continued. It was made of stacked stone, roughly hewn, but no less effective for its crudeness. Unless the builders had completely cannibalized a nearby hill, the stone must have come from far up river, and at great expense.

The hill itself had also been worked. A slowly spiraling road led from the base all the way to the castle at the top, completing a total of seven revolutions as it did so. At first, Kellacun thought it wasteful, as a short series of switchbacks could have achieved the same and reduced the time carts took to reach the summit. But then she remembered the floodgates on the plains. The spiraling road was yet another defense. Invaders would have to march all the way around the hill seven times, all the while being inundated with arrows, crossbow bolts, rocks, burning oil, and whatever else the besieged defenders had stockpiled in there. Building a ramp would prove difficult, considering the hill would be surrounded by a shallow sea.

Kellacun began to wonder what sort of a man would go to such extreme lengths to defend himself from attack. In the final tally, Nalir was still mostly just a swamp. The planning of the kingdom and keep bordered on a sort of engineering paranoia. What exactly was King Hector afraid of. Or, an even more worrisome possibility, what was he hiding?

The time for idle speculation was over as she reached Perseverance Street. Sure enough, on the corner sat, slouched really, a building claiming the mantle of Bog Water. Age hadn't yet had time to account for the structure's unhealthy slant, which was instead owed simply to sloppy craftsmanship. Standing outside the door were several patrons who stood just as straight as the bar they'd just exited, despite it being mid-afternoon. One of them busied himself redistributing his share of ale into the gutter.

Kellacun's eyes rolled back far enough to see the roots of her hair. *Why does it always have to be the most disreputable, unstable looking tavern in the city*, she thought. *Surely there's a nice art museum somewhere? Maybe a sports arena?*

Annoyed, yet undeterred, she walked straight and true for the bar. The shudder-style door swung inward at her push. Pipe-smoke stained windows allowed little light to enter along with her, but judging by the shabby state of the occupants, that was probably a good thing on balance. Her eyes adjusted quickly, and Kellacun scanned the room for her quarry. It didn't take long to find him.

Sitting at a table in the corner, loudly regaling an audience of empty whiskey bottles, sat the single ugliest man Kellacun had ever laid eyes on. Every adjacent table was empty. She pushed past several gawking onlookers and came to a stop in front of the half-blood.

"I'm looking for a man named Bladewright.

You him?"

The lump of man stopped in mid-sentence and turned his face to consider her. Short tusks protruded from his lower jaw, leaving a convenient path for a thin line of drool. "Exchuse me, Madam, but I wassin the middle of a story."

"Story time's over. I'm looking for work."

Bladewright tipped his chair back on two legs and smiled crookedly. "Oh really? Well then, little lady, you can go to work clearing out my empty friends here and getting me fresh ones." He took in a deep breath in preparation for a hearty laugh, but Kellacun didn't offer him the chance. She snapped a foot out hard, cracking one of the chair legs and sending the half-orc tumbling backwards into the wall. He rolled with the collapse and thrust his boots against the floor trim. His feet planted, he launched himself towards Kellacun like a stone from a catapult. Shocked at his reflexes, Kellacun barely ducked the attack in time to watch him sail overhead, then she rolled under the table and kicked it over, putting a two-inch thick oak barricade between them.

Standing fast, Kellacun drew both of her enchanted rapiers as Bladewright regained his footing. The bar fell dead silent, until only the pure tone of her still-ringing swords filled the air. Everyone in the room stared. Not at her, not at the half-orc, but at the silver blades in her hands. Several palms gripped the pommels of their own swords and daggers, while intent eyes watched for her next move.

Bladewright broke the silence. "You have a lot of

nerve coming into Nalir brandishing Al'Kalidian steel. Where'd you get those swords, girl? You elf kin?"

"Not likely. These are trophies, from the first assassins I killed. The *first*, not the *last*."

Bladewright's eyes narrowed. His stance was solid, betraying no trace of the many bottles of whiskey he'd drained. "I'd call you a liar and have these men kill you, if you didn't move so damned fast. How do you know my name?"

"A mutual friend told me I might find an old, wore-out merc down here who might get me noticed with Hector."

"That's right fancy, girl. This 'friend' got a name?"

"Not that I recall, but he did say 'Long live the Undaunted.'"

"Well," Bladewright smirked. "That shortens the list rather considerably. Turn that table right and grab a chair. Let's talk business."

The hands in the bar left their pommels and returned to their tankards as Kellacun sheathed her swords. She pushed the table back over as Bladewright sat down. "So, you're looking for merc work? Why should I hire you?"

"Because I've killed a pair of Al'Kalidian assassins after my scalp. That should be enough resume for anybody. Better question is why should I work for you?"

Bladewright apparently found this very amusing.

"What's so funny?" Kellacun demanded.

"I'm just trying to figure out if your bravado comes from an excess of bravery, or for want of brains." He swiped a fresh whiskey bottle from the clammy hand of the barkeep and ripped out the cork with his teeth. "Our friend didn't share many stories with you, I see. If he did, you wouldn't have to ask about my qualifications. These elves you killed, what were they wearing?"

"I . . . um . . . "

"What, don't remember? Let me save you some time. They were wearing black capes with silver trim, right?"

"How do you know that?"

"Because your accent is from up river, pretty far. I'd guess you're from Central City or thereabouts. Al'Kalidians wandering that far north are only going to come from one cast. The black cast is real, bottom of the barrel scum. They're the lowest knot on the Al'Kalidian rope. They usually get fed up with being treated like dogs after a hundred years or so and strike out on their own as sell-swords, trading on the fearsome reputation of the Al'Kalidian name with people who don't know any better.

"So, yeah, you killed a couple dregs, which was no small feat I'm sure. But don't confuse them with actual Al'Kalidians. Hell, the real elves would probably thank you for your trouble before killing you to take back their steel. You may be tough enough for Central City, but face it, you're out of your element here. Which makes you a risk for a business-minded man such as myself."

Kellacun had to work to maintain a proper facade of indignant affrontery, but she knew Bladewright had struck an accurate blow. She knew nothing of this city, the kingdom, or its people. She hadn't spared a thought of what drawing Al'Kalidian swords would mean to the locals. At least she knew what dangers waited for her back home, but here, she could be killed without a moment's notice, and without ever knowing why.

Not that she was going to let that stop her.

"I admit that I'm new here, but I'm not new to the job, and I learn quickly. I have . . . unique skills to offer."

The half-orc snorted. "I've sailed with an albino Minotaur. How 'unique' can you be?"

Kellacun narrowed her gaze and let her voice drop to a whisper. "Pray you never have to find out."

Bladewright shook his head and took a long, slow pull of whiskey. Once the burning liquid had run its course into his stomach, he leveled his yellow eyes at Kellacun like a pair of javelins. "Tell you what, I'm going to hire you. If you're as good as you boast, you'll be a good investment. If you're just bluffing me, your death will be very satisfying. Either way, I come out ahead."

"Sounds fair," Kellacun said with far more confidence than she felt. "What's the job?"

"There's no reason for you to know, but we have a very serious hog problem out on the plains."

Kellacun nodded. "I've heard as much, wild pigs are wrecking the crops, so what?"

"Ahh, you've heard of the piglets, not the sow. The momma pig is a monster, and she needs killin'. Oh, and one crack about it being a relative of mine and I'll split your skull right here."

"Wouldn't dream of it," Kellacun lied smoothly. "But it's just a pig, there has to be someone in the castle who can kill it?"

"Three volunteers thought so, too. All we found were their boots. This isn't just a slab of bacon, the sow weighs over fifty stone. Hector is tired of wasting good men on her, so he asked me to find some poor sap to do the job. You're the sap of the day."

Kellacun ignored the jab. "How much coin?"

"No coin. Think of this as an audition."

"No coin? I have to eat!"

"Well if you succeed, you'll get fifty stone of pork, ham, and bacon. That should keep a skinny little waif like you fed for months."

Kellacun crossed her arms. "That's not funny."

"Why? You're not one of those meatless, grass-eating weirdoes, are you?"

"No, I'm one of those 'weirdoes' who likes to get paid for their work."

"Coin's not all you want. You want an audience with King Hector. That only happens if I sign off on your mettle. You want to prove you're good enough? This is how you're going to do it. So, what's it going to be, sister?"

"What do you think of Mr. Fellax's story?" Dolan laced his fingers together and leaned back in his chair.

Pavco picked a fingernail. "I think he's either an incredibly brave soldier, or an incredibly brave liar."

"There is great risk of death in either case, that is true. But of the particulars, do they hold up to what you know of your . . . people?"

"Mostly. The only way I've seen, without silver or enchanted weapons of course, to truly kill a 'rat is to cut off their head. I suppose braining one with a big enough rock would probably do the same job. Makes one wonder, though."

"Wonder what, exactly?"

"How a man who can barely walk can get close enough to a 'rat to hit her with a damned rock. Especially *that* 'rat."

"Yes, but keep in mind that Kellacun was wounded. Your man Grascon did accomplish that much.

"True, I s'pose. Still, awful convenient that he was the only survivor. No one else to counter his story."

"And convenient that he destroyed her head, making it useless for identification purposes," Dolan added.

"*And* that he was too wounded to drag the body back out with him, but not so badly that he couldn't get back to the city himself."

Dolan sat in contemplation for several long moments. "What of the ear, then?"

"See," Pavco settled deeper into his chair, "that's the one thing I can't ignore. It's a 'rat ear, no mistake, and the dry blood on his dagger also matched. It's not like she'd have just let him saunter up and cut off a trophy, is it?"

"That would seem, improbable, yes." Dolan scratched at his goatee. "So you believe Mr. Fellax?"

"Not as far as I can piss pudding. She may have cut it off herself to try and trick us. If that's the case, he's working with the bitch. I'd kill him first chance, if it were me."

The duke couldn't help but smile. "While such tactics may work among criminals, Pavco, in polite society it is considered bad form to execute people for doing their jobs well. The rest of my guards are already hailing him a hero. Killing him now would not help palace morale."

Pavco waved a chubby arm dismissively. "Naw, you've got it all wrong. Don't scrap him right away. Pay him his bounty, let him run around town for a couple months, drinking and whoring to his heart's content, then when everybody's forgotten about it, he can die accidentally, see? Maybe even have one of my boys do it, then Mr. Fellax can die bravely in the line of duty, the public gets its hero's funeral, and you are out a potential assassin."

Dolan smiled thinly. "I'm impressed, Pavco, you're starting to think like a noble. Consider it a contract, then. Mr. Fellax will have a very happy, very short, rest of his life."

"Fine, fine. What about Kellacun? How can we be sure she's dead?"

"Simple, my dear thief, we wait. If she hasn't come after me again in the next few months, it's because she's feeding beetles."

Chapter Four:
Hunting for Ham

Kellacun's boot sunk halfway to her knee into the stagnant, brown water of the bog. It oozed over the top of the boot's leather, soaking her foot in the warm, sickly liquid.

"Wonderful." She tried to pull her leg back out, but the muck seemed to constrict, holding her foot fast. Annoyance and a sprinkle of panic took hold, and she jerked up with all of the enhanced strength her 'gift' had bestowed. Mercifully, her foot came free, and for a moment Kellacun smiled in triumph. Until she realized she was staring at her toes. Her boot remained mired in the morass.

"Naturally!" she groaned as she grabbed the boot and gave it a tug. But it was hopeless. She decided it was probably ruined and took off the other one, then tossed it in the mud. She'd never liked those boots anyway, they didn't fit her right. And as long as she was telling herself comforting lies, she would soon have enough coin to have custom boots cobbled from the most expensive and durable leather.

She stood and started down the 'trail' again. Her bare feet moved much more easily over the soggy earth, and it wasn't long before she was glad to be rid of the boots. The trail she was following was little more than a line of wooden planks that had been laid down in the swamp. Reeds and cattails had grown up around the planks, giving passersby some limited footing.

Kaplan strut proudly ahead of her. Despite the cat's immense size, her four large paws splayed out and kept her from sinking very far. Kellacun hadn't needed to wait very long for the cat to find her once she left the city. Their quarry's known range was actually closer to the grain fields than they were now, but that was the point. She was trying to circle around behind the sow. It was a cunning beast, and had become very weary of the trails coming from the city. But no one came from the wild swamps, for reasons that were becoming all too obvious to her.

Kellacun had spent the rest of the day talking to local hunters trying to get an idea of how to tackle the beast. "Don't" was the advice she received most frequently, followed by, "Settle your affairs." The outpouring of support warmed her heart. It wasn't until she'd learned of a hunter who now relied on a cane to walk, courtesy of the sow, did she find someone to take her seriously. Revenge was a powerful motivator, one she could relate to only too well.

After the death of her parents, visiting her own brand of justice against Duke Dolan had become an all-consuming obsession. Pursuing it had already cost her Joshua's love, her innocence, and as she walked across the putrid swamps of Nalir, it nearly cost her life.

If her attention hadn't been turned inward, she

might have noticed that Kaplan had stopped. She might have spotted the chunks of wood that marked the trail suddenly took on a bumpier, one might say scaly texture. But focused as she was, she was wholly unprepared when the 'trail' snapped up and threw her high into the air.

Suddenly very alert and living in-the-moment, Kellacun's head swiveled around, desperately hunting for the ground. She managed twist her body and get her feet under her just as she hit the earth, and immediately wished she hadn't. The soft mud of the bog swallowed her feet up to her mid calves before finally absorbing her momentum. One exploratory tug and she knew she was stuck. Kellacun craned her neck back to see what had tossed her like a doll, and immediately wished she hadn't.

She'd never seen anything like the beast charging towards her. It slithered across the mud like an enormous snake, yet also pushed itself along on four trunk-like legs. Its leathery skin was covered bumps, knobs, and plates of armor. But its most impressive, imposing feature was the enormous maw bearing down on Kellacun's head. In an instant, her entire world was filled with the rows of yellowed, peg teeth, pink tongue, and the smell of rotting meat.

Unable to run, and about to be snapped in half, Kellacun panicked and drew her rapiers. The blades had barely cleared their scabbards when the monster's jaw snapped shut around Kellacun's chest and waist. Her demon-skin armor kept the stout teeth from reaching her insides, but the strength behind the beast's bite was immense. She didn't dare exhale; there was no chance of drawing another breath.

Her head still free, Kellacun peered straight into the protruding, coppery eye of the monster. But her arms were thoroughly pinned, there was no way to fight back against the power of the monster's jaws.

A glint of metal at the edge of her vision drew her attention. It was the tip of one of her rapiers, sticking straight out of the beast's lower jaw. Kellacun's head spun around to the other side and, sure enough, the other blade had erupted from the top. She had drawn them just in time for the monster jaws to clamp down on them like a pin cushion.

Kellacun desperately twisted the handles of the swords, wrenching her wrists while the blades sliced through scales and muscle as bright red blood started to flow over the metal. At first, the beast tightened its grip, trying to end its prey's struggling. The sound of two of her own ribs snapping echoed through Kellacun's skull. She fought against the waves of pain and nausea that threatened to crash over her. Stars flashed across her vision as what little air she'd kept in her lungs grew stale.

Then, with the same suddenness as the attack had begun, the nightmare beast relented and opened its jaws wide. With a violent shake of its mighty head, Kellacun was thrown clear and landed heavily in the mud, flat on her back this time. She pulled in a ragged breath, cut short by the stabbing pain of the broken ribs. Only then did she see Kaplan, harassing the beast from behind, swiping at its tail with her claws and snarling like a hellhound.

Miraculously, Kellacun still held both of her trophy rapiers. With her head still spinning, she sat up and took a knee. Kellacun got to her feet and sprinted as best as she could over the soggy ground. Her breaths were painfully shallow, and with the mud pulling her down with each step, she could only cover a short distance before the stars returned. With a one deep, stabbing breath, she whistled to Kaplan, who saw that her person was safe and broke free of the fight.

Kellacun, Kaplan, and the monster shared a few moments staring at each other, weighing their options. Kellacun realized quickly that she simply didn't have the weapons or strength needed to fell the monster and decided to go around it. For its part, the beast decided that the pointy little two-legged thing didn't have enough meat on it to justify a chase. The scaly behemoth disappeared into the mud from which it came. Kellacun weakly leaned against Kaplan's soft warm fur and fought tears. Is this what her life had become? How could she live up to her bargain with the Nonul?

Kaplan nuzzled Kellacun with her large furry head. Kellacun felt the looming despair fade. She patted her only friend and struggled to tend to her wounds.

His horse growing tired, Joshua pulled up on the reins and dismounted. The animal's white fur was stained with sweat around the saddle and withers. He'd decided to travel fast and light, forgoing the polished, ceremonial breastplate, gauntlets, and shield that had always accompanied him on his few ventures outside the walls of Central City.

After three full days trekking through the forest and along the river bank, he was now further from home than he'd ever been. Traveling alone and far from home, he would make for an inviting ransom hostage for any enterprising criminals who recognized him. Secondly, his quarry had more than a full week's head start. Despite being injured and on foot, she would cover ground quickly. He would need to use every step of the speed in his father's prized thoroughbred if he was going to catch up.

But finally, and most importantly, if he did catch her, Joshua was gambling that being unarmored would signal that he wasn't there for a fight. After their last encounter, Joshua held no illusions about the outcome were he to fight Kellacun for real. Somehow, with shocking rapidity, his beloved, raven-haired mason's daughter had transformed into a remorseless, and highly capable killer.

And he knew who was responsible for Kellacun's horrid transformation; his own father. Joshua found himself in an impossible position, trapped between loving two monsters bent on annihilating each other. His only hope to save them from mutual destruction was to keep them as far apart as possible. Joshua could no longer say for certain what his feelings for Kellacun were, things had gotten much too complicated. But whatever their love had become, he had to convince her to abandon her quest, even if it meant they would never see each other again.

He untied a water-skin from his tack and popped the cork. The horse-temperature water drained down his throat in a most unrefreshing way, reminding him just how far from the comforts of the palace three days travel had taken him. The sun hung low and orange on the horizon.

The road's stones came to an end just ahead of him, terminating abruptly near a series of piers. An assortment of boats, canoes, and barges were lashed to them, but it seemed that their owners had already turned in for the night. All but one of them. A lone man continued to toil away on the deck of his barge, loading cargo in preparation for departure.

"You there, good man," Joshua called out.

The man stood straight and turned in Joshua's direction, but didn't look at him. "I'm sorry, sir, are you talking to me?"

"Indeed. Have you seen a young woman pass through here." He held a hand up to his chin. "About this tall, with long raven hair?"

The old bargeman chuckled. "No, sir. Can't say I've seen anyone like that."

Finally comfortable with the distance she and Kaplan had put between them and the . . . whatever it was, Kellacun peeled the onyx-black armored shirt from her skin. Baring her breasts to an assortment of dragonflies and frogs of the swamp, she probed her rib cage with carful fingers. The fight had left her injured and demoralized. Even free of her armor, she still couldn't draw a full breath.

She gasped a little as her fingers found a tender spot on her side, just out of sight. It was hot and sticky, and when she pulled her hand back it was covered in blood. One of her ribs had cracked and protruded past where she could get a decent look at it. Her healing powers could not get started until it was back in place.

Kellacun muttered a curse and crunched her torso away from the injury. On a silent count of three, she inhaled as deeply as she could, expanding her ribcage out as far as it would go. The stabbing became overwhelming, but she held her breath and shoved the floating piece of rib back into place with a click. Black dots erupted in her vision as red-hot pain washed over her consciousness before darkness greeted her.

Morning approached by the time Kellacun awoke again. She sat up and took an exploratory breath. Much to her relief, the pain had subsided almost entirely. The sun hadn't quite broke over the horizon yet, but with her dark vision, it may as well been the middle of the afternoon.

She took a moment to scan the area for any other nightmarish creatures bent of swallowing her whole, but found only a Kaplan napping contently next to a half-eaten boar carcass.

"Some friend you are," Kellacun kicked the cat on a paw, "wandering off to hunt while I'm lying unconscious in the mud."

Kaplan woke up just long enough to give her an annoyed look, then rested he head on her forearm again. Kellacun then took stock of herself, and realized she was every bit as dirty as one would expect after sleeping half-naked in a swamp. She splashed herself to rinse off the mud caked to her body as best she could, but the water was only marginally less dirty than the mud had been.

With her body still slick, she struggled to pull her demonskin shirt back into place, then strapped her rapiers to her waist. She glanced at her father's sabre lashed to her pack. It was a heavy, unwieldy weapon, better suited for loping off heads from horseback than fighting on foot against a capable opponent. Still, the odds that a wild boar would also be an expert swordsman seemed remote, and the top-heavy blade would be good for slicing through its thick hide.

She tied the sword off around her back and started walking in the direction the village hunters had told her was the sow's domain. Kaplan followed a short while later. They hadn't walked very far before the swamp started to harden up into proper ground again. Here and there, stray crop plants grew wild, their seeds caught on the wind and carried from the fields closer to the coast. Her stomach had been complaining for hours already. She'd come to realize that her rapid healing came at the price of immediate hunger. The wandering crops hadn't yet matured, and she was already out of the hard trail cake she'd nicked from a vendor in town. She regretted not cooking up a piece of Kaplan's evening kill.

The only hunting Kellacun had done in her old life was for fresh tomatoes in the city markets. She didn't know where or how to start looking for a wild pig, even if it did weight half a ton. With no experience to lean on, she concentrated on her senses. She knew what pigs smelled like from farmers bringing their animals to market, so she cleared her nose and let the mingled smells of the swamp fill it.

Hidden among the rotting plants, flowers, mud, and smoke breezing by from Nalir, Kellacun thought she could pick out a trace of swine. It was faint, but definitely present. She sniffed around until the odor became stronger, giving her a bearing to follow. Kaplan trailed behind her, curious about what the funny little creature was going to do next.

The scent trail grew steadily stronger. It was soon joined by a bona fide set of tracks, although they seemed much too small to have come from the monster sow she was meant to kill. Still, hogs travelled in herds, didn't they? It stood to reason that finding one would bring her closer to the sow. With clear tracks to follow, Kellacun broke into a jog, while Kaplan bounded along playfully behind her.

The trail led into a thicket of spiny bushes. Kellacun drew a rapier and slashed a path through them. In a small clearing at the center of the patch, a piglet stared back at her, frozen in terror. It couldn't have been more than twenty pounds, certainly not the gargantuan beast Kellacun was hunting.

The poor thing was actually pretty cute in a muddy, hairy sort of way. But as her stomach reminded her, what the piglet lacked in size, it made up for in deliciousness. It certainly wasn't Kellacun's fault the Gods had conspired against the piglet by making it out of bacon.

She thrust the tip of a rapier at the forlorn creature. It deftly sidestepped the attack and spun around on a hind hoof. Then it tore deeper in the thicket, squealing for all it was worth. Kellacun was about to go after it, but Kaplan knocked her flat on her bottom as the huge feline surged past, completely overcome by the instinct to chase any small, fast-moving objects.

"Don't eat it all!" Kellacun shouted to Kaplan's rapidly retreating tail. She got up and ran down the path Kaplan's body had cleared through the brush. She'd barely gotten her feet up to full speed before running into the cat's immobilized rump. The piglet had stopped squealing, and now stood facing Kellacun and Kaplan with a look that said, *Now you're gonna get it.*

Standing, towering over the piglet was the source of its newfound confidence; the sow. She was as tall as Kaplan, and twice as wide. Foot-long tusks caked in mud curled up from the hog's lower jaw, while black beady eyes stared back at the intruders. The hunters tales had, for once, understated the size of the foe she faced. It was as big as a horse, and the aura of its stench assaulted Kellacun's nose like an unkempt stable at the height of the summer heat.

Fortunately, the sow's eyes bore straight and deep into Kaplan at the moment, ignoring Kellacun completely. While this was good news for her immediate survival prospects, Kellacun was at a loss to how she was supposed to kill the beast. Kaplan was apparently grappling with the same question, as she crouched low and started to growl deeply. Playing her part of the deadly dance, the sow snorted and started to paw the ground, the needle-like hair on her spine standing straight up.

Kellacun decided quickly that she did not need to be in the middle of whatever furball was about to erupt between the two of them and moved to a better position. There, with sweat beading up on her forehead, she waited to see which of the great animals would make the first move.

As it happened, it was the sow. A wave of muscles and fat shot through her bulk as her hind legs dug into the soft earth and threw her forward like a bullet from a sling. Kaplan answered an eye blink later, and the two behemoths collided in a cloud of dirt, claws, tusks, teeth, and hooves.

The force of the blows from Kaplan's paws would snap all but the stoutest men in twain, while the slashes of the sow's tusks would shred any armor short of full-plate. The raw power and brutality of the fight rattled Kellacun to her core. In the last year, she'd fought for her life at least a dozen times. She'd grown used to the rush of battle, the keened senses, the slowing of time, and the heat of the blood rushing to her muscles. But to see a fight like this, no armor, no weapons but what the Gods had endowed them with . . . it was unpolluted, unbridled savagery.

Both combatants threw themselves into the fray

with no regard for their own safety. The fight was pure offense. Yet neither could seem to land a decisive blow on the other. Kellacun could see her cat was wearing down. The bruises and small lacerations were adding up, and the cat didn't have her rapid healing. Every moment that the fight went on, Kaplan would grow weaker from the accumulated blood-loss.

Kellacun knew she had to change the dynamic of the fight, but she had no idea how. Even if she turned full wererat, the hog was simply too much for her. Just like the monster that had nearly eaten her the day before, she could do no more than annoy the beast.

Her eyes darted to the piglet on the other side of the clearing, watching the fight just as intently as she. Her plan crystalized in a moment. While the sow's focus was still on Kaplan, Kellacun sprinted around behind the bushes and grabbed the piglet. She tucked it under one arm and ran straight back down the way she'd come.

"Kaplan!" she cried, hoping the tiger's bloodlust would lift long enough to realize the game was now afoot. The frenzied scream of the piglet stung her ears like a swarm of wasps. Amazing that such a huge sound could come from such a tiny set of lungs. Kellacun looked back to see that she now had the attention of Kaplan and the sow, both of which charged towards her with a purpose.

Just as she'd hoped, Kaplan was gaining ground just a little faster than the giant hog. She was lighter, and her broad paws gave her better footing over the soft earth. But the sow still moved shockingly fast.

Getting caught on open ground was not an option. She felt Kaplan's footfalls approach. Kellacun looked back and grabbed a handful of hair on Kaplan's shoulder, then used her momentum to swing herself up and onto the tiger's back, squealing piglet still securely clamped under her other arm.

Kellacun dug her heels into Kaplan's sides, spurring her onwards down the trail. A thunder of mud-slapping hoofbeats kept pace behind them as the sow continued her pursuit. Kaplan quickly carried them back onto the fetid plains of the swamp. Even with the extra weight of Kellacun and the piglet, Kaplan's paws kept her from sinking very far.

The sow was a different story. Her hooves kept getting caught in the brackish mud. Kellacun managed to slow Kaplan down, deliberately keeping the distance between them and the hog from growing. She needed the sow to keep coming.

The giant hog didn't disappoint. The cries of her panicked piglet kept her surging forward through the muck. The chase continued deeper onto the plain. Kaplan began to pant heavily from the strain. Fortunately, the finish line was in sight.

With the exhausted sow still in tow, Kellacun took the screaming piglet in both hands and hurled it towards a familiar patch of disturbed earth. As she'd hoped, the hog abandoned the chase and headed straight for her offspring, and into Kellacun's trap.

A spray of mud and clumps of grass exploded into the air as a giant, toothy mouth erupted from the swamp. The hog tried to stop, but her enormous girth carried too much momentum and she slid forward on her belly. The monster that had nearly swallowed Kellacun the day before surged forward and snapped its jaws shut, then thrashed its head from side to side with dismembering force.

Kellacun declined to watch. The sow's death was violent, but mercifully short. Sated from its half-ton pork dinner, the swamp monster sank beneath the mud once more. Gingerly, Kellacun approached and fished out a hoof the size of Kellacun's own foot that had snapped free. Shreds of muscle tissue and sinew hung from the morbid trophy.

Kaplan, never one to let meat go to waste, had already finished the piglet by the time Kellacun turned around. She tucked the proof of her kill into her pack, mounted her tiger, and headed back to Nalir.

Chapter Five:
A Rat in the King's Court

The mutilated foot landed heavily on the small table in front of Bladewright, knocking over his whiskey glass and sending a miniature tidal wave of the amber liquid spilling into his lap.

"You're buying me another drink," he said gruffly.

Kellacun matched his tone. "And you're buying me dinner."

The half-orc picked up the shattered leg-bone and sucked out the marrow. Kellacun's stomach churned in protest, but her face betrayed none of her squeamishness.

"So," Bladewright waved the foot in the air, "what's this then?"

"What do you think? Proof I finished the job."

"Where's the rest of it?"

"Unavailable."

Bladewright laughed. "You mean to tell me you tore that whole boar apart by yourself?"

"I may have recruited some help."

"I suppose you ate the whole thing and shit it back out again, too."

"No, hence why you're buying me dinner, then

taking me to the King, as agreed."

"Oh, now, slow down tough girl. There is a time and place for everything."

Kellacun slammed her palms down on the table. "I just spent two days trudging through a Gods-forsaken swamp, where I had the pleasure of almost getting killed twice. The time, half-blood, is now, and the place is the palace. Can you get me an audience with the king, or do I have to slice my way through his guards?"

Bladewright's rage at the blood insult she'd leveled sat in near perfect equilibrium with his admiration for her rank audacity. If she realized how close she'd just come to being cleaved in half, it didn't show.

"That was the agreement, wasn't it?" Bladewright said through clenched teeth. "But you're not going looking like that. Go clean up, make yourself presentable. Surely there's still some trace of a lady hidden under all that grime."

Kellacun bristled. "I'm trying to get hired as a scout and assassin, not a harem girl."

The half-orc cackled in laughter. "I doubt you're in any danger of being added to Hector's personal collection. He has *taste* in women. But, there are still appearances to keep up and respect to be given. You want to work for a King? Look the part. Now, off you go, before I decide to become annoyed."

She set her eyes. "Dinner first."

"Whiskey first."

"Done."

Read more about the adventures of Kellacun in the rest of The Wererat's Tale III: The Collar of Perdition by Patrick S. Tomlinson